DEDICATION

To everyone who chooses to smile.

PLAYING IN THE RAIN

A Novella

JANE HARVEY-BERRICK

HARVEY
BERRICK
PUBLISHING

CONTENTS

PROLOGUE

THE REASON I'M STANDING HERE WITH MY BOARDING PASS IN my hand, waiting to fly 7,000 miles to an adventure in a new country, is because of him.

He crashed into my life, like an ocean wave out of a millpond sea. He changed everything.

I'm gripping my boarding pass for dear life, and I'm choked with nerves by what I'm about to do.

But then I see him. I think I see him. Across the crowds of people, swirling among the human river, a flash of blue eyes. That smile, that love of life, a shock of black hair. I see him and then he's gone, lost somewhere in the sea of faces.

And I smile.

CHAPTER ONE

THICK, HEAVY DROPS OF GREASY RAIN, FUNNELED BY THE windshield, bounced off the hood, streaming in rivulets down the misty glass.

I couldn't see out. My brand new Prius, my energy saving car, didn't believe in wipers that worked while the car idled.

The car may have been stationary, but I was fizzing with angry energy.

I thumped the steering wheel in sheer frustration. Not normally a road rage person, I was mad beyond belief.

What a complete and utter fiasco. I could not believe *that* just happened. Being an intern at Wallman & Wallman was my dream job. Had been my dream job. But that douchebag made it perfectly clear that he'd only given me the position if I gave *him* the position he wanted, which was me on my knees. Which turned out to be blowjobs in the Boardroom, because it was his company and he was the boss.

Yeah, there are laws against it, but who'd believe me? No one. Absolutely no one. I'd been played by the ultimate player, and I'd lost.

I told him where he could stick his job, blow or otherwise, and it was in a place where the sun didn't shine.

He fired me on the spot, because unlike him and his subtle,

solo harassment, I told him where he could go in the main reception area at work.

I told him he was a delusional asshole and *he* fired *me*.

Not only was I now jobless, I had rent due on my new apartment, and no friends to turn to in a city where I'd lived for only four weeks. And now I was stuck in a traffic jam, with my gas tank perilously close to empty. Stuck in a line of cars, shiny metal boxes going precisely nowhere. In the rain. In the pouring, pounding, lashing rain.

It wasn't supposed to happen like this. None of it was supposed to happen. This was southern California, for crying out loud. It wasn't supposed to rain at all. I'd seen the movies —wall to wall sunshine.

But oh no. God hated me so much that my life had crapped all over me and now it was freakin' raining.

I'd been so excited when I'd been offered this position. All my hard work throughout four, dreary years of college, working towards my goal of becoming a Certified Public Accountant. I'd hoped to start paying off my student loans as soon as I'd got my license; planned a stable future, a secure life on my own terms and my own merit.

Finally, I'd be able to do something that made my dad proud. It wasn't easy being the youngest in a family of over-achievers, and he'd always regarded me with an air of faint disappointment. That, along with low expectations.

Dad had been reluctant for me to move so far from home, so far from his influence and that of my older sisters, but I'd ignored all his well-argued concerns. And even though he thought it was a mistake, he'd paid for me to fly out here; and for the deposit on the expensive apartment with the good security, video entry and 24/7 doorman that he'd insisted on; and my shiny eco-car car that he'd paid for.

It was supposed to be an exciting new world.

It was supposed to be my time.

My turn.

I'd never felt so miserable. *And it was still raining.*

That's when I saw him.

A blur of movement caught my eye as the rain on my windshield gave the illusion that I was underwater. He was running, which I suppose is what people do when they're caught in the rain. A huge furry dog was running next to him, matching his long, even strides, both of them drenched and dripping, their feet splashing through puddles, raindrops running off their faces.

His white t-shirt had become transparent and clung to his muscled chest, and I could see the rapid rise and fall of every breath. He raised his hand, the tendons flexing in his forearm as he pushed his dripping black hair out of his eyes.

And then he'd passed me, leaving a glimpse of his tight butt in a pair of running shorts, and long muscled legs striding out. All of those things caught my attention, but what totally captured and held it so I couldn't look away was the huge smile of pleasure on his face.

He was soaked to the skin and smiling so wide I could see his even white teeth, grinning like a loon, like he was *enjoying* the rain.

"What an idiot," I muttered to myself, locking my doors just in case lunacy was contagious.

The runner slowed down, turning into the entrance of the park opposite where I was trapped in my car. He bent down to lever a tennis ball from the dog's mouth, and his t-shirt rose up his back, showing his trim waist and lean hips. He threw the ball like he was pitching a baseball, and the mutt barked and leapt after it, his thick tail windmilling crazily.

The dog bounded back, barking around the ball wedged in its mouth, leaping up and leaving muddy footprints over the man's t-shirt. He threw his head back and laughed, wrestling the saliva-coated ball from the dog, and threw it again.

He didn't even try to shelter from the rain. He was playing with the dog—playing in pouring the rain.

And then his head snapped up and I swear he looked right at me, as if he'd felt the weight of my amazement. I sunk lower in my seat, refusing to meet his gaze, staring stonily ahead, but not before I noticed that the crazy guy was freakin' beautiful.

Not just plain old handsome—but beautiful. High cheekbones, lips that were full and pink from exercise, and stunning pale blue eyes, framed by long dark lashes. Model perfect white teeth, and a body built for…

Oh God, I was overheating, because if ever I'd seen a body built for sin, that man had it. Although now I'd seen his face full on, he was younger than I'd originally thought; my age perhaps.

The traffic began to move forward, tearing my thoughts from the beautiful man who was standing in the rain, still watching me.

I let the Prius crawl a few feet up the road. Red tail lights flared in front of me then vanished again, and I was about to pull away for a second time when someone banged on the passenger window, making me squeal in fright.

It was him, and he was smiling at me, gesturing for me to put down the window.

I stared back, my mouth hanging open in shock, then I jumped again when the car behind me honked loudly.

"Patience is a virtue, asshole!" I yelled to the rear view mirror, then flushed bright red when I saw my gorgeous stalker grinning.

He gestured again for me to roll down the window. I pressed the button to open it a crack, and he slid a piece of paper toward me, winked, then continued with his run, the ugly fur ball loping beside him.

I read the smeared writing, the ink bleeding into the wet paper. I'd expected a name and a phone number, or maybe the name of a bar and a time, but all the paper said was,

You're beautiful

That was it. Nothing else. Just two words.

The car behind me honked again and I dropped the note, inching forward with the traffic.

♡ ♡ ♡

I couldn't park outside my building. Of course not. Why would my luck change on such a shitty day? I had to run nearly two blocks in my favorite Louboutins—the ones that I'd intended to afford with my first pay check. Or my second. Soon, in any case.

I'd have to phone Human Resources to find out what I was entitled to. After all, I'd worked at Wallman's for a month—I must be owed something.

I grabbed a clean towel, rubbing it over my hair as I trailed through the apartment, finally dumping it over a chair to pull the sodden newspaper out of my purse. I concentrated on trying to turn the damp pages without tearing them, hoping that there'd be something in the Employment or even the Want Ads. Right now, I'd take anything, even another waitressing job, like the dozens that had gotten me through college. Anything so that I didn't have to go crawling to my dad for money. So I didn't have to prove what he already suspected about me.

As I turned the pages carefully, a piece of paper fluttered to the floor. I picked it up, the stranger's note, then screwed it into a tight ball, meaning to toss it into the garbage.

Something stopped me. I hesitated, reading the innocent words again, and I smoothed out the scrap, ironing it with my fingers and put it onto the kitchen counter to dry.

I needed a drink. It wasn't something I did often, but I had learned the benefits of insanely strong alcohol on occasion.

I'd hidden a bottle of tequila behind a packet of dry pasta, and I coughed slightly as the liquid scoured my throat, but it had the calming effect I craved. I felt my cheeks flush, both from the drink and the memory of the last three hours—the hours when a huge sinkhole had appeared in my world, and I'd fallen right into it. It had been a long time since I'd lost my temper like that in public. I'd worked so hard to rein it in over the last four years.

I looked over at the piece of paper again, miffed that the mystery man had cut and run without leaving a way for me to get in touch with him. But then again, when was the last time somebody had done something nice for me, just for the hell of it? When was the last time *I* had done something nice? It had been a while

And without my permission, a smile twitched at my lips.

It *had* been kind of sweet. Crazy, but sweet. And there was no doubt he was hot. Maybe it was better this way; I could just remember it as an intriguing and perfect encounter on a really shitty day, rather than another random guy who'd hit on me.

I knew that men found me attractive. It wasn't my fault that I fit the dumb blonde stereotype. Yeah, I had big boobs and long, blonde hair. But that didn't make me a bimbo. My 4.0 grade point average proved that. I'd worked my ass off in college. I *deserved* to have a great job.

Depressed by the thought that I no longer did, I peeled off the tight, black pencil skirt, and rain-soaked gray silk blouse, changing into a pair of comfortable sweats and old sneakers.

I'd planned on ordering Chinese, but knowing how my bank account languished dangerously close to zero, I decided to forego easy, and headed back out to the local grocery store instead, trying to save a few bucks.

I loaded up with healthy food, and stuffed a bar of chocolate in at the last moment. I really wanted to buy myself a bottle of wine, but decided that $9.99 was more than I could afford right now.

On the way back, I passed an elderly woman who seemed familiar. As I hurried past her, head down, unwilling to speak, I realized that she lived in my apartment building. She was battling to carry a bag of groceries and an umbrella.

Damn it!

I looked over my shoulder, watching her, stoic in her struggle. Maybe it was the random act of kindness from my mystery man, but I turned back, and found myself offering to carry her groceries as well as my own. Why did it have to be today that somebody did something nice for me?

"May I help you with that?"

She looked afraid for a moment, and I felt a pulse of irritation that my gesture had been misconstrued.

But her expression morphed into surprised wariness.

"I live in your building," I said.

She nodded and ventured a small smile.

"I know, dear. I've seen you. I tried to talk to you the day you moved in."

I frowned. *Really?* I didn't remember that.

"Do you need any help with your groceries?" I asked again, trying not to snap at her as she gazed up at me myopically.

"Thank you, dear," she said, at last.

She handed me the paper sack. Darn it was heavy, and awkward to manage with my own purchases. And then we proceeded to move at the pace of an arthritic snail as we made our way toward the apartments.

My hair hung in wet clumps and I was soaked to the skin, again. Why was doing a good deed such hard work?

But then she smiled and thanked me, and I enjoyed the swell of pleasure that warmed my insides.

See, I'm a nice person. I help old ladies, even if I am jobless, an irresponsible dreamer, just like my father always said.

♡ ♡ ♡

The next day I decided to walk to the park, hoping to see my mystery man, but of course, he wasn't there. I might even have thought that I'd invented him if it hadn't been for the scrap of wrinkled piece of paper that I'd stuck into the frame of my bedroom mirror.

I sat on one of the benches, lost in thought, feeling sorry for myself.

Today the sun was shining, beating down in a glorious display of warmth that made the damp grass hiss and steam.

A woman with a toddler and a small, yappy terrier headed toward the children's play area. I watched as she tied the mutt to the swings' frame by its leash, the beast staring morosely at the empty stretch of grass where mystery man had thrown balls for his dog.

The toddler shrieked excitedly as his mama pushed him

higher and higher. His little face was red from yelling and a small slug's trail of snot pulsed from one nostril. But he didn't care and his mama didn't notice; they were too busy being happy, the swing arcing through the air.

It occurred to me that one dog walker might know another, especially if he came to this park every day. It was worth a shot, even at the risk of some mild humiliation when I had to explain what—or who—I was looking for.

I smiled at the woman as she slowed the swing, and I bent down to stroke her scruffy dog. It growled, showing sharp yellow teeth, and I stepped away quickly. The woman gave a short, embarrassed laugh.

"Sorry about that. Ludo isn't very friendly. He's just old and grouchy. Like my father-in-law," she muttered under her breath.

"No problem," I said, side-eyeing the dog as it sniffed at my ankles. "Um, I wonder if you can help me? There's a guy who comes here—he's about six foot or maybe a bit taller, black hair, blue eyes, and has this huge dark brown dog, like a Newfoundland or something. I'm not sure, but it's massive and hairy. I don't suppose you know him, um, them?"

She smiled knowingly.

"Uh-huh, I sure do. That's Cody." Then she placed her hands over her child's ears. "He's *hot*, if you know what I mean."

"Oh definitely understanding you," I agreed, with a conspiratorial smile.

She sighed and fanned her hands in front of her face before she started pushing her son again, rocking him more gently now. "God, if I was ten years younger—and not happily married..." Her words trailed off as her eyes took on a dreamy expression.

"So, he comes here most days?" I prompted her.

"Not every day. I think he just moved to the area." She smiled. "But I've seen him here a few times. Mostly in the afternoons. Maybe if you hang around now you'll see him."

I grinned back at her.

"I might just do that. Thanks."

I found another bench to sit on and stretched out my legs, hoping to catch some sun. I'd been so busy for the last month that I'd barely had a moment to take advantage of being in sunny San Diego. I was feeling pale and in extreme need of working on my tan.

While I waited, I pulled out my phone to check my messages.

Chloe wanted to know how my job was going. I deleted that one. Time enough to talk to my big sister. She was always in my face, wanting to know my business.

I also deleted a text from Emily who questioned why I hadn't gone home for the Fourth of July parade, and would I be home for Labor Day, Thanksgiving and Christmas.

No, no and no. What the hell was she doing asking me all that when it was only mid July?

I deleted three more messages from my other sister, Julie, and one from my dad, all asking the same questions: how was the job, was I managing, when was I coming home.

I shoved my phone away, scowling at the blameless blue sky. Sighing, I decided I really needed to send out my résumé to a few places who might be hiring. No more time for sitting in parks hoping to ogle hot guys.

And then I saw him.

And he was even more beautiful than I remembered.

CHAPTER TWO

HE HADN'T SEEN ME, SO I WAS ABLE TO WATCH WITHOUT HIM knowing.

Truthfully, I was staring. He looked even more incredible without the veil of yesterday's rain. Today, his hair was slicked back with sweat, and the white t-shirt had been replaced with a pale blue that matched his eyes.

As I continued to stare, he grabbed his shirt by the back of the neck, yanking it roughly over his head, and tossing it onto the grass.

His furry friend bounced up and down, clearly recognizing this as playtime. I watched the man pry the tennis ball from the beast's jaws, ignoring the accompanying drool, and threw it 20 yards.

Mystery man was ripped. I could count his abs as he bent and stretched, and the muscles in his back rippled every time he threw the ball. His skin was smooth and tanned a deep golden-brown, accentuating those extraordinary pale blue eyes against his black hair.

He was graceful, too: every movement purposeful, with a hint of restrained power.

After a few minutes, the hound flopped at his feet, worn out by the heat and its own shaggy coat. Mystery man poured some water into his cupped hands and let the dog lap at it messily.

The man—Cody, as I now knew him—looked up and saw me, pausing in surprise, then flashing his meltingly-beautiful smile.

As he walked towards me, my heart gave a hopeful little leap.

"Hi," he said. "You're the girl in the car."

"Yes," I squeaked, annoyed that my voice was an octave higher than usual, just when I'd wanted to sound husky and sexy.

"You look different out of your business clothes."

His words, which could have been innocent, took on a sultry tone as he continued to gaze down at me.

I felt my cheeks heat as I squinted up at him, shading my eyes from the sun, trying to figure out how to answer, but he saved me the effort.

"Can I buy you an ice cream? There's a guy across the park that makes awesome frozen yogurt."

"Are you hitting on me?"

The words blurted out in an embarrassing gush of sound.

He grinned. "Well, yeah, I guess! Pretty girl, beautiful day, awesome frozen yogurt—definitely one of the good days. I'm Cody."

He held his hand out to me then stared at it in dismay.

"Uh, that's not such a great idea. I'm pretty sure Oscar drooled on me." He wiped his hand down his shorts, then turned and called over his shoulder. "Oscar, come here, boy! Come say hi."

The beast reluctantly heaved itself upright and padded over, breathing doggy breath into my face, then sat on my foot, a furry ton weight.

"Aw, he likes you!"

"Yeah, it's, um, mutual. Can you get him off me? I can't feel my foot."

He grabbed a handful of fur and tugged Oscar an inch, allowing me to wriggle my sandal free.

He grinned, completely unabashed.

"What's your name, pretty girl?"

I was slightly annoyed by his over-confidence, but decided I'd give him the benefit of the doubt. For now. But only because he was mind-bendingly hot, and his bare chest was stopping me from thinking straight.

"Ava."

He smiled again, softer now.

"So, Ava, can I buy you that frozen yogurt?"

I nodded and stood up awkwardly, relieved when he pulled his t-shirt back on. Too much desirable male flesh was beginning to freak me out. It had been a while.

Oscar huffed out a frustrated sigh, hauling himself upright again and plodding along behind us.

"Shouldn't you put him on a leash?"

Cody laughed out loud, and I found myself smiling for no reason.

"Nah. He's too hot and tired to run off, aren't you, fella?"

Oscar gave a feeble wag of his tail, showing no inclination for anything livelier.

"But they have leash laws."

"Are you going to report me?"

I was stung. "No! Of course not! But somebody else might."

He glanced around.

"Don't think so. Most people around here know Oscar— they all know he's harmless."

"How do you know so many people when you just moved here?"

He raised his eyebrows. "Who told you that?"

My face flushed bright red, giving me away.

"I haven't seen you here before," I said, with a lift of my chin.

"Maybe you're new," he countered. "I haven't seen you before yesterday either, and I think I'd have noticed."

"I've been here a month," I defended.

"So long?"

He was laughing at me, which made me a little mad.

Especially because I never got flustered around guys. Until now. The thought made me defensive.

"I have to go," and I turned around to leave.

He laid a warm hand on my arm, making my skin tingle pleasantly.

"Don't go, Ava. I'm just messing with you. I'll be good, I promise. So will Oscar. See, I'll even put him on a leash."

He clipped a long red leash to Oscar's collar. The beast raised his heavy head and stared at Cody, a wounded expression on his solemn face, then promptly laid down.

"Come on, Oscar! Move!"

Cody tugged at the leash, but the huge hunk of fur wouldn't budge an inch.

"I don't think he likes being on a leash," I said, trying not to laugh.

Cody grinned at me.

"Nope. Hates it."

"Will he move if you leave it on?"

"Probably not..."

I sighed, pretending to sound resigned.

"I guess you'd better take it off then."

He winked at me, and unclipped the leash.

Oscar grumbled under his breath then lurched to his feet again.

"You're a faker, my friend," Cody said, rubbing the dog's massive head. Oscar's tongue lolled out of his mouth, giving the impression that he was smiling.

We walked in silence for several minutes, and I wondered again what I was doing here.

"How come you're not working today?" Cody asked, eventually.

I bristled instantly. That was a *very* sensitive subject.

"How come *you're* not?"

He shrugged, but didn't look at me.

"I don't want to work."

15

"That must be nice," I said, waspishly.

He grinned, amused by my sharpness.

"Yeah, it'll be great. I'm going to make a wish list of all the things I've ever wanted to do, and I'm going to do them all this summer."

I glanced at him to see if he was joking, but he looked serious.

"What sort of things?"

"Well, I haven't written them down yet. But ... I've always wanted to get a tattoo."

I couldn't help looking at his perfect, unblemished skin, wondering how a tattoo would look.

"Really? What would you get?"

He pointed to his left shoulder. "A yin and yang symbol."

"Oh, I thought you'd get something tribal."

"Why would I do that?"

I shrugged. "Those are popular, right?"

"Yeah, I guess. But I want one that means something to me."

"So what does yin and yang mean to you? You don't look Chinese."

He laughed again, flashing his perfect teeth at me. *It must be nice to be so happy*, I thought.

"Not so as you'd notice. Nah, it's about opposites interrelating, natural duality: light and dark, fire and water, sun and moon, male and female, life and death." He smiled again. "And it'll look cool."

I snorted and raised my eyebrows.

"So you'd mark your skin permanently just to look cool?"

"I can't think of a better reason. Why, what would you get?"

"I don't think I want a tattoo—I'm scared of needles."

He tried not to smile, but failed. "Nah, you'll be fine. I'll hold your hand."

I blinked and looked away.

"Come on, Ava," he said, dropping his voice and upping the

sexiness factor by ten. "I've shown you mine, so now you've got to show me yours. What tattoo would you get?"

I took a deep breath to calm my raging hormones.

"Well, in the extremely unlikely scenario that I'd get one at all, I'd get the astrological sign for Pisces, because my birthday is in March."

"Do you believe in all that shit?"

He was annoying me again.

"You're allowed to have some far Eastern symbol for 'duality'," and I raised my hands to make air quotes, "but I'm not allowed to have my birth sign?"

He shrugged and grinned, a small dimple popping up in his cheek. "Fine—you can have whatever tattoo you like. Where would you get it? On your...?" and he looked down at my butt.

"No! On my wrist. So I could cover it up with my watchstrap if I wanted to."

He looked puzzled. "Why would you get a tattoo then cover it up."

Because my dad would go ape shit, but I wasn't about to tell him that.

"Just so."

He raised his eyebrows and smiled, but didn't push me.

After he'd bought two frozen yogurts—and an orange ice for Oscar—we sat on the grass under the shade of a large mulberry tree to eat them.

"What else have you got on your wish list?" I asked, as I licked my frozen yogurt (which was both delicious and addicting).

I tried to ignore Oscar's hopeful expression as he begged for mine, too.

I caught Cody's eyes flicking up from my mouth as I spoke, and I could have sworn that he blushed.

So, I wasn't the only one who was getting flustered! The thought pleased me too much.

I needed to find a new job, not get involved with someone who couldn't even be bothered to look for work, no matter how hot he was.

He busied himself pulling a small notebook out his runner's belt bag, and wrote the numbers one to 10 vertically.

At number one he wrote:

1 Get a tattoo

"What about you?" he questioned. "Is there anything you've always wanted to do?"

I thought hard. There was one thing…

"No, it's silly."

"Go on," he encouraged me, as I sat chewing my lip.

"Well, I've had this thing about dolphins, ever since I saw *Flipper*. I'd love to go swimming with them; in the wild, if possible."

"Actually, that's pretty cool," he said, and made a note at the second point on his list.

2 Swim with dolphins

"But that's my wish, not yours!"

"What? We can't share the same wishes?"

"Well, if you really want," I said, smirking at him, "I give you permission to share my wish."

He winked, and then wrote something else on his list.

"What did you put?"

He angled the notebook toward me.

3 Get drunk and high in Tijuana

"Seriously? That's on your summer to-do list? That's not very mature."

"Sure, why not? I'm a guy: we like to do stuff like that and I've never done it. Wanna come with me?"

"No!" I said, immediately.

He grinned. "I'll work on you. You'll say yes eventually."

I shook my head, but didn't bother to argue.

"Okay," he said. "Your turn: add something to the list."

I thought for a moment, then wrote:

 4 Have a star named after me

He raised his eyebrows, looking impressed.

"That's a really good one. What made you think of it?"

I wasn't sure I wanted to tell him because the reason was personal, but then again he'd shared his wish list with me, even if it was kind of silly so far.

"My mom died when I was seven. I didn't really understand what that meant; I just knew that she was gone. Dad told me she was in heaven with the stars, and when I looked up at night, I could see her twinkling for me. I know that sounds dumb, but I believed it at the time."

"It's not dumb at all—it's beautiful, Ava."

He spoke with such sincerity that I was a little embarrassed. I handed the notebook back to him.

"Okay, your turn. Make another wish."

"Easy," he said, writing rapidly.

 5 Ride through Monument Valley

"Really? Why do you want to do that?"

He shrugged. "It's just something that I've always imagined: being outdoors, not shut in surrounded by walls, somewhere really amazing. I used to watch Westerns with my dad when I was ... when I was younger. It looked like an interesting place to go."

"Yeah," I nodded. "I can understand that. I've always wanted to go camping—sleep under the stars. Not in a tent, but under the stars. My family never did anything like that. I didn't even go to summer camp."

"That's easy to fix," he said, then wrote on the list:

 6 Sleep under the stars

"Maybe we could combine that with riding through Monument Valley?" he suggested.

I shook my head and laughed.

"I don't think so!"

"Why not?"

"Because ... because it makes no sense."

"I think it makes perfect sense," he argued, a huge smile on his face. "We both get to do our wishes, and we don't have to do them alone. It'll be fun!"

"You know, you're kind of crazy. You don't even know me!"

"Well, you don't look like a homicidal maniac."

"That's what you think; I could have been yesterday."

"Why? What happened?"

I was annoyed with myself for having brought it up.

"Nothing. Forget about it. What else do you want to do?"

He stared at me for a moment, frowning slightly, then let it go with commenting further.

"Oh yeah, the next one's a good one."

7 Jump out of an airplane

I read it with a shudder.

"You've got to be joking! Why would anyone jump out of a perfectly good airplane?"

He smiled so wide, his dimple popped out again. It was very distracting.

"If your chute opens, you know that God loves you."

"Yep, I was right the first time: you're crazy."

He nudged the notebook towards me.

"Go on. Your turn now."

"Nope, I'm not putting anymore wishes on the crazy guy's list."

He shook his head in mock sadness. "Well, I'll just have to fill up all the spots by myself."

"Feel free," I said, magnanimously.

He wrote for a minute, then handed me the notebook.

" 8 Meet a Native American medicine man

" 9 Help in a homeless shelter

" 10 Have sex on the beach

"What do you think?" he said, when I hadn't spoken for half a minute.

Truthfully, I was beginning to wonder if he had multiple personality disorder.

"Um, interesting mix," I said, as honestly as I could.

I could tell he was disappointed by my lack of enthusiasm, so I tried to make light of it. "Sex on the beach is very unusual in California," and I rolled my eyes to emphasize the sarcasm.

He smiled, but I caught the glint of desire in his eyes as he returned my look.

"Maybe, but I haven't lived here very long."

"Yeah, right!" I scoffed. "You could walk into any bar you like and not go home alone!"

He cocked his head to one side. "What makes you say that?"

"Well, look at you! You're hot and you've got that dimple— gotta tell you, bud, it's all workin' for ya!"

His smile was surprisingly shy. "You think I'm hot?"

"Hell, yeah!"

He looked down at the list as if he was studying it.

"So do you wanna?" he said, at last.

"Want to what?" I asked, warily.

"Do you want to do the list with me? I mean, not the sex on the beach thing, obviously. Unless you wanted to. Shit, that didn't come out right. Um..."

His cheeks were bright red, and it was my turn to laugh.

"I'm not jumping out of an airplane either."

He looked up at me gleefully. "But you'll do the rest?"

"Maybe."

"That's not a no."

"This is completely crazy! I don't know the first thing about you, and you definitely don't know me!"

He shot me a sideways look. "Don't you ever just want to say to hell with it? Take a risk once in a while?"

God, yes! I was so sick of being sensible. And where had it gotten me? Fired from my first real chance at a job.

I held out my hand and Cody took it, his face lighting up with delight.

"But I'm still not jumping out of an airplane."

He laughed happily.

"We'll work up to that one, too."

CHAPTER THREE

My phone buzzed with a text message, waking me from a deep and satisfying sleep.

I pulled the annoying gadget toward me and squinted at it with one eye.

> Wake up, pretty girl! #2 on the list!

I sat up straight, suddenly wide awake. Oh God! What was number 2? I couldn't remember—it better not be jump out of an airplane because there was no way I was doing that.

My phone buzzed again.

> Are you up yet? Flipper is waiting!

That got my attention. Oh wow! Number two was *swim with dolphins!*

> Seriously?

> Yes! Text me your address. I'll pick you up

I sent a quick reply then ran to the shower. By the time I came out, I had two more texts from Cody.

Wear a swimsuit

I'm outside

God, I hoped this wasn't a mistake. I'd given him my address, and I hardly knew the guy! Was this a date? We hadn't discussed it, and I wasn't sure how I felt about that.

I peeked out of the window with my towel wrapped tightly around me, and saw a dark blue Silverado pickup with white racing stripes. I'd never have figured Cody for something like that—it was more the sort of thing guys back home drove.

He saw me and waved impatiently.

I ducked down, feeling my heart pounding. *What the hell was I doing?* No, I'd had enough of doing what I was supposed to and playing it safe. I was going to do this—whatever *this was*.

I rummaged through my dresser, looking for my one-piece swimsuit, but all I could find was my bikini. When I heard him honk the first time, I pulled it on, cringing at how much boob was spilling over the top.

By the second honk, I'd dragged a brush through my wet hair and yanked on a pair of cut-offs and strappy t-shirt.

By the third honk, I was racing down the stairs and Cody was leaning against the door of his truck grinning at me.

"It's rude to honk like that when you go to pick up a girl!" I snapped.

"Made you move your butt though," he snickered. "Come on, I'm taking you to breakfast."

My face fell. "I thought we were going to swim with dolphins?"

"We are, but SeaWorld doesn't open until 10AM."

"SeaWorld?"

He pulled a face. "Yeah, sorry. I couldn't find anywhere with wild swimming that was close enough. But this should be cool. We'll be in the pool with the dolphins and get to feed them and play with them and stuff."

He looked so worried that I felt guilty when he'd planned this specially for me.

"It sounds great," I reassured him. "I'd never have gotten around to doing it by myself. So where are you taking me for breakfast? I could go a plate of home fries, scattered, smothered and covered."

"What the heck is that?" he laughed.

"Hey, don't knock it! That's Carolina food at its best: home fries, smothered in onions and bacon, covered in American cheese and served with two scrambled eggs. Mmmm!"

He grinned, looking relieved, and that darned dimple popped out again.

"Well, I was thinking more Muffin Heaven. They do the best blueberry muffins *ever*. Wait till you try them."

Cody was right. Even though the small family bakery was only four blocks from my apartment, I'd never been there. The smell of fresh baking had my nose twitching, and Cody looked like he wanted to fight his way to the front of the short line.

I couldn't help smiling.

"What?" he asked, glancing over his shoulder.

"You've got the exact same look on your face that Oscar had yesterday when he was eyeing up my frozen cherry yogurt."

Cody laughed. "Yeah? But with less drool, I hope."

"Hmm, well, this friendship is fairly new so I'll take a rain check on that. By the way, what sort of dog is Oscar?"

"He's a Bernese Mountain Dog, but not pure bred. I think there's some Newfoundland in there, too."

"Does the father have visiting rights?"

Cody grinned. "I don't think he was the responsible kind."

"Uh-oh, one of those hit-it-and-quit-it types. How old is he?"

"I'm not sure. Four or five. Getting on for a big guy."

Cody's smile faded.

"You're not sure how old he is?"

"Well, he's not mine. He belongs to a neighbor. I just walk

him sometimes. He's good company—you know, the strong silent type."

"Hmm, makes a change from the chatty, crazy type who writes messages to random strangers."

He laughed, then looked at me quizzically.

"Which do you prefer?"

"The strong silent type, but the crazy type's growing on me, too."

"Good," he said, throwing a heated look that shut me up.

When we got to the head of the line, Cody ordered two coffees and six blueberry muffins.

"How many people are you feeding?" I asked, incredulously.

"I'm hungry," he defended. "You can have two."

"What if I want three?"

He gave me puppy-dog eyes. "You'd eat my muffin?"

"Just asking for an equal share, mister."

"Fine," he said, with a smile. "I'll watch you eat three muffins, then I'll watch you throw up."

"Wow, how'd you get to be so charming?"

"Practice."

"I bet you say that to all the girls."

"Only the pretty ones who want to eat all of my muffins."

"Just my fair share!"

We sat in his truck, sipping scalding hot coffee and eating our blueberry treats. I managed two-and-a-half, but only because I was determined not to be a girl about it.

Cody snatched the remaining crumbs out of my hand and stuffed them in his mouth, a look of triumph on his face that didn't match his bulging cheeks.

"Oh my God! You look like a hamster."

He mumbled something I couldn't understand, then swallowed and proceeded to lick his blue-stained fingers clean.

I was mesmerized by his pink tongue winding around his fingertips, wondering what else he could do with it.

He caught me looking and raised his eyebrows.

I should have looked away but his expression became serious. For a second I thought he was going to kiss me, and I really, really wanted him to. But then he cleared his throat several times before looking away and starting the truck's engine.

The awkward moment passed when he turned on the radio and a John Denver song blared out.

Cody started singing along, his voice strong and surprisingly tuneful, with a rough, sexy edge. I could imagine him fronting up a rock band—he was certainly hot enough.

"How come you know all the words to that?" I asked, when it had finished.

He grinned, completely relaxed again.

"It's my mom's favorite," he smiled. "'Some days diamonds, some days stones.' It's about making the most of what you get in life; you know, life deals you lemons so make lemonade and all that happy shit."

"Very philosophical."

He shrugged. "I like it."

We drove in silence the rest of the way to SeaWorld, each lost in our thoughts, although I saw him glancing across at me a few times, like he wanted to say something but wouldn't or couldn't.

At the aquarium, we were taken to a small classroom with three other people—a mom and two children—and given a short lecture on dolphins, their behavior and habitat.

Cody was as excited as either of the kids, and eager to get in the tank with the dolphins.

"We're going to meet a thirty-year-old dolphin named Mavis," said the trainer. "She's very friendly and loves being around people."

"Wow, thirty years old," Cody said, softly. "She's almost a senior citizen dolphin."

The trainer smiled.

"Don't let her hear you say that; Mavis is very spry!"

We were shown to the changing rooms and given lockers

for our clothes. I felt self-conscious in my bikini, but the mom who was with me sighed enviously.

"What I'd give to have your figure. But having two kids ... well, let's just say that gravity isn't kind."

I smiled and thanked her.

"Your boyfriend is a sweetheart," she said. "My two little trouble makers are quite smitten."

I knew the feeling.

We made our way out to the pool area to collect our wetsuits.

Cody was chatting with the trainer, and even though I'd already seen most of his body when he wore his running shorts, I couldn't help but enjoy the very pleasant scenery.

His mouth dropped open when he saw me, and I watched his eyes travel across my body with obvious appreciation. I shivered under his gaze, and was both relieved and disappointed when we were handed our wetsuits.

We splashed the water with our hands, our greeting to Mavis. She swam toward us and I held my breath as she brushed against my hand. Her skin was slightly rough, slightly rubbery, but her touch was gentle. She circled us slowly, coming close in, then pushing away.

"She's checking you out," said the trainer. "Just let her swim around you a few times and get used to you."

"She's smiling at me!" the little girl giggled excitedly.

"Dolphins look like they're smiling, but it's their behavior that tells you how they're feeling. Yep, she definitely likes you!"

Mavis swam toward us again, then nudged me with her head, pushing me into Cody.

"She thinks you make a cute couple," whispered the mom.

I felt my cheeks heat up but Cody laughed and put his hand around my shoulder, pulling me in closer.

I felt warm all over: from the sun, from this wonderful experience, and from the man standing next to me, smiling like I was the best thing he'd ever seen.

We stayed an hour with Mavis, playing with her, feeding

her, sharing her environment, and getting our pictures taken with her.

I was totally blissed out by the time we finished; deeply relaxed in a way I didn't understand, but that was entirely new.

We stayed a while, looking at some of the other sea creatures, but it made me feel sad seeing animals in captivity, even large, beautifully maintained aquariums like these. They weren't meant to be caged; they should be in the ocean, free, living their lives. Not here, no matter how well they were looked after.

Eventually, we headed for one of the cafés and sat chatting in the sunshine.

When we strolled back to Cody's truck, he opened the door for me.

I couldn't remember the last time I'd enjoyed myself so much on a first date. Was this a date? It felt like one, but without the usual awkwardness. Maybe we were just two people making our wishes come true.

As Cody climbed into the truck, I leaned over and kissed his cheek.

"Thank you. That was amazing. One of the best things I've ever done in my life. Thank you for taking me."

He smiled and looked down to where my palm was resting on his knee, and he threaded his fingers through mine.

"I'm glad you liked it," he said, squeezing my hand gently before letting go. "Want to cross something else off the list?"

"What did you have in mind?"

"Number one."

Uh-oh.

"You mean...?"

"Yep, tattoo time!"

"Oh, I'm not sure about this."

"It'll be fine, Ava. I'll go first so you'll see that it's okay. But only get yours if you really want to; we can still cross it off the list if just one of us does it."

I agreed reluctantly, a queasy feeling in my stomach, and I was regretting the tuna sub that I'd eaten at SeaWorld.

He drove into a part of the city that I didn't know, following the instructions of his GPS, and finally pulling up outside a store front that had the words 'Propaganda Tattoo' painted across the large window.

I peered out anxiously, and Cody had to coax me out of his truck with a promise of cookie dough ice cream later.

He held my hand, rubbing his thumb across my knuckles to soothe me, then led us into the tattoo shop. I was surprised by the clean, open-plan space; I'd expected something grungy and dirty.

"May I help you good people?"

A huge man with tattoos scrolling up his neck and thick arms walked toward us. I hid behind Cody while they discussed his yin and yang tattoo.

"Your girlfriend can wait out here or come and watch," he offered.

Cody winked at me, but didn't correct the man's assumption.

"Do you want to watch?" Cody asked, looking concerned as the blood drained from my face.

"Um ... I'm not sure."

"He'll be fine, honey. Maybe you could hold his hand for him—it's always the tough guys that turn out to be wusses."

I laughed shakily but followed them into the booth.

Cody sat in something like a dentist's chair while the tattoo artist who called himself 'Monk' wiped the top of his arm with antiseptic and shaved it carefully. Then he traced out the transfer and positioned it on Cody.

"Last chance to change your mind, man."

Cody smiled at me. "Nah, I'm good."

The buzzing of the tattoo gun made me feel faint. Cody didn't move, but I saw a vein pulse in his neck, and his jaw showed tension. Without thinking, I pulled his hand into mine and held it tightly. He blinked in surprise, then smiled at me.

Fifteen minutes later it was done. Cody's skin looked a little pink around the edges, but otherwise not as raw as I'd expected.

The yin and yang design was fresh and sharp-edged, and was about the diameter of a baseball. It looked pretty good.

Monk smothered some gel over Cody's new tattoo, and covered it with something that looked like saran wrap.

"You gonna get a tat, little girl?" asked Monk, turning to me.

When he smiled I noticed that he had a tooth missing. I couldn't help wondering whether an unhappy customer had punched him.

"You don't have to, Ava," he said, gently.

Why was I such a chicken shit? I raised my chin sternly.

"No, I want to get one, too. I want to remember this day."

Cody's smile was so wide, he glowed with happiness.

"I'll never forget it," he said, staring into my eyes.

I leaned forward and his eyes darkened, the atmosphere heating between us, until Monk cleared his throat.

"So what do you want, honey?"

I blinked a couple of times, embarrassed by how I was behaving, but nothing about today had been usual.

"I'd like the astrological symbol for Pisces, please."

"Not a dolphin?" Cody smirked at me.

I ignored him and showed Monk where I wanted the tattoo.

"Just here."

I unstrapped my watch and showed him the place on the inside of my wrist.

"Sure, honey. But just so as you know, it'll hurt some because you don't have much flesh and it's near to the bone."

I'm pretty sure every drop of blood left my face and I swayed slightly.

"Um, Ava? I'm not sure this is such a great idea," Cody said, worriedly.

"I'll be fine."

My voice sounded faint even to my own ears.

Monk shook his head and sighed, before settling me in the chair and cleaning my wrist.

He was right: it did hurt, and the vibrations of the tattoo

gun made me feel like my teeth were rattling. I couldn't look, but Cody held my hand until it was finished.

"All done."

I stared at my wrist, slightly appalled. I looked like I'd been branded, but I was also rather pleased with myself, and with the small symbol that was now indelibly inked onto my skin.

Once again, Cody refused to let me pay, pulling out his wallet and handing over a bundle of bills.

"How can you afford to do all this stuff when you don't have a job?" I grumbled. "Don't you have college loans to pay off or something? Or are you just rich?"

Maybe the ink had gone straight to my brain, because I knew I was being rude. Cody didn't answer immediately, an oddly opaque expression clouding his face.

My knees buckled as I left the shop, and I gripped onto the doorframe when a wave of dizziness seized me.

"Whoa! Are you okay?"

Before I could answer, Cody swept me up into his arms and carried me to the truck. My head felt like it was revolving slowly; but resting against his firm chest, focusing on the steady beat of Cody's heart, I began to recover. I became hyperaware of the faint smell of chlorine on his skin, a hint of the cologne that he'd worn earlier, and the subtle scent that was all his own.

I was just beginning to enjoy the experience, when he placed me carefully onto the passenger seat.

"How are you feeling now?"

I laughed awkwardly.

"Embarrassed, mostly."

A soft smile highlighted the relief on his face.

"Maybe I should take you somewhere and feed you."

"Are you kidding? You've already bought me a tuna salad sub and two muffins. I'll be the size of a water buffalo if you carry on like this."

"Two-and-a-half muffins."

"Whatever!"

"Well, I did promise you cookie dough ice cream."

I sighed. "Yes, you did. But I'm paying."

"I like it when you boss me around," he said, with a wicked grin.

I rolled my eyes, but couldn't entirely hide my smile.

We drove out to the Moo Time Creamery in Coronado and sat in the sun, enjoying our cones.

"You never answered my question," I said, licking the last ice cream drips from my fingers.

"Which one?" laughed Cody. "Some people around here talk non-stop."

It was true: we'd been chatting away like old friends. Everything with Cody was easy. Almost everything. I was still wondering why he hadn't tried to kiss me.

"Are you rich?"

He laughed huskily.

"Not so as you'd notice—rich in experience, maybe."

"So how can you afford all this? I mean it's really nice of you…"

"Really, Ava, don't worry about it. I've got some money saved up. I've been planning this for a while now."

"Yeah, but I can't pay you back. I … I kind of quit my job, or maybe I was fired."

His voice was full of concern.

"But … you're not sure?"

"Well, I was working as a paid intern at this Accounting firm—it was supposed to be my big start. But then my boss, who also co-owns the company, he suggested that if I could 'help' him, he could 'help' me, if you get what I'm saying."

Cody's expression darkened and his full lips were pulled into a hard, flat line.

"Say the word, Ava, and I'll go beat the ever-living shit out of that bastard. I mean it. He can't get away with that."

He looked so furious that I knew he'd do it if I said the word.

"The guy's a douche, but I'm not going to let him ruin everything," I sighed, trying to believe the words I was saying. "I really like living out on the west coast. I'll find another job."

Eventually. "But I can't pay you back yet, "and I don't like being in debt."

"You're not in debt to me," Cody replied, almost angrily. "I'm doing this because I want to—and I really enjoy your company." He looked at me sideways. "It's much more fun doing this stuff with someone."

"So you really are just going to have an endless summer of gratification?"

He smiled widely. "It sounds even better when you say it like that."

I shook my head, even though I was smiling at him.

"And then what? Will you look for a job after Labor Day?"

He shrugged, dismissing the subject. "I'll worry about that when the time comes."

I huffed in annoyance. "Has anyone told you that you're very evasive when you want to be?"

He looked surprised, then shifted uncomfortably. "Um, no. Not before today."

"Well, you are."

He didn't reply, and I couldn't help wondering about the possible reasons why.

"You're not married, are you?" I asked, bluntly.

It seemed a reasonable question, particularly based on recent experience with a serious misreading of my douchebag ex-boss.

Cody's eyebrows shot up and a loud laugh erupted from him.

"No! Definitely not married."

"Kids?"

He shook his head.

"Jeez, Cody, you don't make this easy. Do you have a girlfriend? Are you seeing anyone?"

His eyes met mine as I frowned at him.

"Only you," he said, then picked up my hand and gently kissed my knuckles. "Okay?"

"Okay," I said, happily.

Then one more thought occurred.

"Are you on parole?"

He grinned across at me. "Hmm, good question."

"Are you going to answer it?"

"No, I'm not on parole."

And then he muttered something under his breath that I couldn't hear.

CHAPTER FOUR

IT HAD BEEN A PERFECT WEEKEND.

Almost perfect. Why the heck hadn't Cody kissed me yet? I wanted to kiss him, but because he hadn't tried, it made me think he just wanted to be friends, and that held me back from leaping on him. Gah! He was so confusing.

But now it was Monday, and I had to go find a job.

I was lucky to get called for interview by one of the small coffee shops where I'd left my résumé; happy to be offered work, but less happy because they could only give me two shifts a week: Mondays and Tuesdays, starting immediately.

There was one piece of good news: Wallman's agreed to mail me a severance check. That meant I wasn't completely destitute, although I seriously needed to think about moving out of my expensive apartment and finding somewhere cheaper. Just what I didn't need; another upheaval in my life.

I didn't hear from Cody all day, but every time my wrist rubbed against my apron, my new tattoo reminded me of him. I really hoped this wasn't going to be something I'd end up regretting.

Toward the end of my shift, I was feeling rather sorry for myself. I hadn't gone through four, long, boring years of college to become an accountant, only to be back waiting tables *again*.

I was tired, and my whole body ached from the soles of my feet upward.

I was pulled from my gloomy wallowing when my phone buzzed in my pocket. I looked around surreptitiously to see if my manager was watching me before I checked the message.

It was Cody, and he was asking to meet up.

A dizzy happiness bloomed inside me, and I sent him the coffee shop's address, saying I'd be off in half an hour. Then I hurried to the bathroom to survey the damage wreaked by a nine-hour shift.

Hmm, not too bad considering. Nothing a comb, lipgloss and quick squirt of perfume couldn't fix. That would have to do. Besides, Cody had seen me in an unflattering wetsuit the day before—it didn't get much worse than that.

I served a couple more customers before clocking out and collecting my purse from the tiny break room. When I came back, two of my new co-workers, college students Shelly and Rachel, were staring across the café and giggling behind the coffee maker; ogling Cody, who was scanning the room, looking for me.

"That boy is fine!"

"Oh, definitely hot. I'm going to talk to him."

"Bitch, you are not! I saw him first."

"Sorry, ladies," I said with a smile, as I sailed past, "he's taken."

Disappointment twisted their faces, and they both shot me angry looks.

They were right, though: he did look fine, and I wondered if he'd dressed up for me.

He was wearing dark wash jeans that hung off his hips, and a white button down shirt. The contrast against his tan skin and black hair was stunning. He was so beautiful he could have made a fortune as a model. I wanted to capture the way he looked there and then, and keep it forever.

But when he saw me, a huge grin lit his face, and *that* was the memory I fixed in my mind. He walked toward me, and for a moment I thought he was going in for a hug, but then he slid his hands into his pockets and rocked on his feet, still smiling widely.

Throwing caution to the wind, I wrapped my arms around his neck and planted a loud kiss on his cheek. He looked so surprised, I wanted to burst out laughing. But instead I grabbed his hand and pulled him out of the café.

"Just marking my territory," I said to him.

His look of confusion was adorable.

"My co-workers were trying to decide which of them was going to hit on you. I thought I'd save you from them."

He grinned down at me, and squeezed my hand.

"I think I need saving more often."

"I'm sure you do!" I laughed. "God, I need a drink after the day I've had. There's a bar across the street that still has happy hour. I'll buy you a beer with my tip money. And I won't take no for an answer."

He shook his head, looking uncomfortable. "Can we just go for a coffee?"

"Are you serious? I've been smelling coffee all day. I'm craving a glass of ice-cold beer."

"Um, I can't go in a bar."

"Why not? Don't you drink? You can have a soda…"

He shook his head again. "No, it's not that…"

"Oh shit! You are on parole, aren't you!"

My eyes widened in panic.

He gave a small smile. "I don't have fake ID."

"What?"

"I'm not 21, Ava."

"Oh." I paused and looked up at him, taking in his smooth skin, and the faint promise of day-old scruff. "How old are you?"

His cheeks reddened and he stared at his shoes.

"I'm 18."

What?

I was staring. I was definitely staring. My eyes swept up and down his body and came to rest on his beautiful face.

"Holy shit! You're kidding me! I'm practically robbing the cradle!" I dropped his hand in shock. "Really? You're only 18?"

He smiled nervously. "That's why I want to go to Tijuana. You can drink there when you're 18."

I was stunned. I couldn't believe that this fine hunk of man was four years younger than me. He seemed so mature; more mature than the college guys I'd dated, that was for sure.

I tried to laugh off my shock. "You must be the only 18-year-old who doesn't have fake ID."

"Never got around to it."

We looked at each other awkwardly, unsure what to say.

"So, you haven't been to college?"

"Nope."

"And you live ... do you live at home?"

He nodded. "Yeah, with my mom."

Visions of creeping into his room to have my wicked way with him, then being interrupted by his *mom* filled my brain.

"Okay, this is weird," I said, trying to get my head around the idea.

"It doesn't have to be, Ava. Nothing's changed."

"Um, yeah it has! I'm dating a guy who isn't old enough to enter a bar!"

He surprised me by grinning, making that darned dimple pop out.

"We're dating?"

It was my turn to be horribly embarrassed.

"Oh, shit. That just slipped out. No, of course we're not dating; we're friends."

His smile faltered.

"I'd like to take you on a real date, Ava. Let me take you to dinner, right now."

I twisted my purse in my hands, confused and slightly annoyed.

"I'm still the same person I was 10 minutes ago," he said, softly. When I didn't respond, he sighed. "Or we can just be friends."

Would it be *so* bad dating an 18-year-old? After all, I wasn't *that* much of a drinker. And it wasn't like he couldn't have a beer if he came to my apartment.

But then I thought about what my sisters would say; and my dad. Oh God, what *wouldn't* he say? I was a complete chicken shit and I needed time to think about it.

"I think we're better off as friends," I said, bluntly.

His shoulders slumped a fraction, and I felt horribly guilty for leading him on then refusing to see it through.

"We can still hang out," I said brightly, then cringed at how fake I sounded.

"Sure," he said, the smile not reaching his eyes.

If possible, I felt even worse now.

"I'd better go," I said, feeling miserable and alone.

He reached out to touch my arm then seemed to think better of it.

"Let me take you to dinner, Ava," he pleaded. "As friends. You've gotta be hungry after doing an all-day shift."

"As friends?" I clarified.

"Yeah, whatever. Friends."

Doubtful this was a good idea, I climbed in his truck, breathing in the smell of dust, old leather and Cody's cologne that was already familiar, and I relaxed immediately.

"I like your truck," I said. "It makes me feel safe?"

"Just what every guy wants to hear," he said, shaking his head in mock sadness.

I smacked his arm lightly. "You know what I mean! It feels like a tank, like you could just drive through anything in this."

"I'm still not letting you get behind the wheel," he laughed, rehashing our argument from the day before. "You drive a Prius. It's about a tenth the size of my truck."

"Is not!"

I pretended to be annoyed, but there was something about Cody that wouldn't let me stay angry with him. Besides, I wasn't really mad. I wanted to be, because he hadn't told me his age. It honestly hadn't occurred to me that he could be so young. My friends from back home would tease me mercilessly, but that would be nothing compared to what my family would say.

A small voice of rebellion whispered, *They don't need to know.*

Oh God, I was being so shallow and insecure—I really hated myself sometimes.

We pulled up outside a pizza parlor and he held open the door for me as we walked in. I couldn't help noticing that the wait staff (including one obviously gay guy) were eyeing Cody with interest. I couldn't blame them.

The hell I couldn't! He was with me, friends or not.

We were shown to a table by a *very* attentive hostess who suddenly seemed to have developed an interest in Silverado pickups. I counted to twenty, then sent her away to summon a waitress.

I realized Cody had no clue that she was hitting on him. Even though he seemed so confident, he was actually rather shy around women. Now I knew he was only 18, it made a little more sense. Or maybe not. What was wrong with the girls at his high school? Were they all blind with no taste for hot guys?

And why was he so different with me? Why had he given me that note when he'd been playing with Oscar in the rain?

While we waited for our pizzas, Cody pushed a thick envelope toward me.

"What's this?"

He raised his eyebrows. "Why do people ask that when all they have to do is open the envelope?"

"Smart ass," I snapped, making him laugh.

The first piece of paper I pulled was headed, *International Star Registry*.

My eyes shot up to meet his.

"Oh my God! Did you do this?"

"Uh yeah, I did. You're not mad at me again, are you?" he asked, warily.

My eyes got a little dewy. "You really named a star for me?"

His shoulders relaxed and he smiled. "Yeah, I got one for each of us. They're in the Andromeda constellation, because, um, 'Andromeda' means 'Princess'. I got one for your mom, too. But I didn't know her name, so her star is 'Ava's mom'. I hope that's okay. And we got neighboring stars ... so you can't get rid of me now."

I couldn't stop stupid tears leaking from my eyes and making my mascara run.

"Oh, look at the state I'm in," I choked out. "I must look like a raccoon."

"Yeah, but a really cute raccoon."

He scooted around the booth and pulled me into a hug.

There was nothing boyish about the way he held me, or the kisses he dropped into my hair as I continued to make a wet patch on his shirt. His arms were strong and warm, his body firm beneath the brushed cotton, the muscles in his thigh bunched up against my leg.

Eventually, I managed to stop crying, and gratefully accepted a handful of paper napkins from him.

"God, I'm so sorry," I sniffed. "I'm really embarrassed."

"Don't be," he murmured, stroking my hair.

"It's just been a really strange few days. But this is one of the best parts. Thank you so much for doing this, Cody."

I pulled away from him slightly, and he dropped his arms. I immediately missed the feel of his body against mine. I asked myself again, *would it be so wrong to date Cody?*

The arrival of the pizzas provided a good distraction, and I dug in hungrily. Cody seemed to prefer to watch me eat rather than feed himself. I was too hungry to care.

"Well, you've organized three awesome items on our summer wish list, I guess it's my turn now," I said, contemplating whether or not I could eat a fifth slice of pizza.

"Are we going to be jumping out of an airplane?" he teased.

"No chance—no matter how much you try to sweet-talk me." I paused. "Don't look at me like that. You make me feel like a cougar."

"You can dig your claws into me anytime."

"Oh, God! That is such a cheesy line!"

He shrugged and grinned. "I'm 18. It's what you expect, isn't it?"

"You don't have to prove it!"

"Why not?"

"You're such a guy! I guess it's true that boys mature more slowly than girls."

"You like it really. Maybe I'll stay 18 forever."

"Nobody can do that. You have to grow up sometime."

"Nah. I think I'll skip that phase."

I rolled my eyes, and stuffed a slice of his pepperoni in my mouth.

I immediately regretted it, because the pupils of his pale blue eyes dilated, darkening with a look that definitely wasn't child-like. He licked his lips, then shook his head and rubbed his temples.

"Headache?" I teased.

He threw me a look that showed he didn't think I was funny.

"Okay, truce," I offered. "How about we shoot down to TJ for the day ... if your mama lets you," I teased him.

He grinned widely.

"Yeah?"

"I'm not saying I'll get high, because I don't do drugs, but if you want to get hammered, I'll be your drinking buddy."

"God, I love y— I love that idea!" he said, happily. "When can we go?"

"Well, I have to work tomorrow, but I'm free the rest of the week. But seriously, won't your mom think it's kind of weird, you going off with an *older woman?*"

He smirked. "I think she'll cope."

"Well, alrighty. Tijuana here we come."

We raised our water glasses and drank to Mexico.

CHAPTER FIVE

WE'D DEBATED ON WHETHER OR NOT TO DRIVE TO TJ. IF WE went on the bus, the wait at the border would be less than an hour; if we drove ourselves, it could be as much as three hours.

Cody decided that he was taking his truck. I decided that I was driving my Prius, and for a while it looked as though we'd been traveling separately. In the end, Cody suggested we flip a coin. I won, and he took it really well—for a guy.

But then we decided that it would be nice to be able to have a drink together, and that we'd take the bus after all.

I said I'd pick him up so we could drive to the terminal together, but he was oddly reluctant to give me his address, saying he'd come to my apartment and leave his truck outside. That seemed so ridiculous that I called him on it.

"And your mom has definitely agreed to this? I'm not going to be accused of kidnapping or trying to corrupt a minor."

His eyes glittered dangerously and he leaned across to whisper in my ear.

"I'd like to be corrupted by you—and there's nothing minor about me."

I couldn't help a guilty shiver of pleasure shooting up my spine as I struggled to play it cool.

"Seriously, has your mom agreed to this?"

I was only half teasing, but Cody looked amused.

"You worry too much. Yes, I've told her I'm going. Yes, I've told her who I'm going with."

I gnawed my lip, still not sure I was convinced.

"Besides," he said, "she's seen pictures of you, so she knows you're too cute and tiny to lead me astray ... even if you are a cougar."

"Excuse me?" I gasped.

I didn't know how he managed to be complimentary and offensive in one sentence, especially in a way that had me laughing and choking at the same time.

He sat back and grinned.

"I've told my *mama* all about you."

"You have?"

"Sure. She wanted to know where I keep disappearing to, so I told her." His amusement softened. "She worries about me a lot."

"Am I going to meet her?"

What on earth was I doing? The whole 'meet the parents' thing was not me at all.

"One day," he answered.

"How about tomorrow when I give you a ride?"

He laughed. "Fine, come to the house. But she won't be awake. She works night shifts."

At least I had his address now. If he was hiding something, it probably wasn't to do with his home after all. Probably.

"Fine!" I grit out. "I'll be there at 7AM."

We'd decided that an early start would give us the best chance of not getting caught at the border for too long.

The next morning, I pulled up outside a small, manufactured home on a quiet street. It was a nice area, but it was clear that Cody and his mom weren't rich. The mystery of how he could afford all this time off deepened. I wondered uneasily if this whole TJ trip wasn't some elaborate scheme to do a drug run.

I wanted to kick myself for that mean thought, but it was there all the same, burrowing away. I felt even worse when he

45

came bounding out of the house, a huge smile on his face and scooped me up into a tight hug.

I couldn't help hugging him back and pushing my face into the soft material of his t-shirt, breathing in his clean, spicy scent.

I felt Cody's heart stutter, and we held each other just a beat longer than was strictly *friendship*. When I pushed him away, I'm sure my cheeks were flushed, and I could see that he wasn't unaffected either. A very solid erection was visible beneath his jeans.

"Sorry," he said, shrugging and avoiding my eyes. "Pretty girl in shorts."

He threw himself in the car then plugged in his iPod, and Lifehouse's *Between the Raindrops* echoed out of my speakers.

I smiled and shook my head. I was about to climb into the driver's seat when I glanced toward his house. I could have sworn that I saw a face peering out between a gap in the curtains. Probably his mom checking on him. Or me.

I headed for the bus station, waiting for Cody to say something, but he was staring out of the window

After a few minutes of awkward non-conversation, I couldn't hold back.

"The day it was raining—why did you give me that note?"

His smile was a little sad as he looked at me.

"You looked like you needed cheering up."

Not the answer I was expecting.

"That's it? Your mission is to go around cheering up random strangers?"

"Sure, why not? I can think of plenty worse ways to spend my time." He looked away, his gaze fixed on the passing scenery of cars and shops. "And I meant what I said. But now I know you, I've changed my mind."

"You ... you don't think I'm beautiful?"

What a letdown.

He smiled and looked across at me. "I know that the outside is just a reflection of the inside."

I laughed shakily. "I think your eyes need checking: I'm

miserable and grouchy and I give you a hard time even when you do nice things for me, then question you like a cop."

He leaned back in his seat, stretching his arms upward, as much as was possible in my small car, and gave me a view of taut, toned stomach as his t-shirt rode up.

"Nah, you've just had a bad few days. Everyone gets down sometimes."

"You don't! You're always happy. It's kind of annoying."

He laughed loudly. "Yeah, don't you just hate that? All those darned happy people! What are they thinking?"

"Asshole," I muttered, even though I was smiling.

His laughter died away and he became serious.

"Life can be shit. You've known that since you were seven. I decided a long time ago that being happy is a choice. When I was 13, someone I knew well got sick with cancer—you could say it was a life-changing experience. So yeah, you can wallow in your own misery and tell everyone what shit luck you have, or you can face it and smile that fucker fate in the face." He paused. "Doesn't mean your luck will change, but you can choose not to be miserable about it."

"Is it really that easy?"

Cody shook his head slowly. "Nope, but it's the choice I make every day."

I phrased my next question carefully. "What made you decide ... to make that choice?"

He closed his eyes briefly. "I'm not going to answer that, because today is about having fun with my ... with my best friend."

I stared at him in surprise.

"I'm your best friend?"

"Truck!" he yelped, gripping his seat hard.

My eyes snapped back to the road and the truck that I'd nearly side-swiped. A blaring horn sounded in my ears as I corrected the steering wheel with a jolt.

"Answer the question!" I croaked, when the immediate danger had passed.

He took a deep breath, and I didn't know if was because I'd

just scared the bejesus out of him, or because he was steeling himself.

"Yeah, you're my best friend."

"Why?"

My question surprised him.

"Why not?"

"No, it's just ... well, what about friends from high school?"

He shrugged. "Lost touch with them."

Well, that was odd.

We reached the terminal and climbed onto our bus, choosing a seat toward the back. It was full of day-trippers and men with buzz cuts who were clearly soldiers or marines, and were excited at the prospect of cutting loose.

It was only a half-hour ride to the border, but once we were there, we ended up in a long line of cars and trucks, all heading south for the winter, like snowbirds.

"Why did you decide to be a CPA?" Cody asked out of the blue.

"Good money; steady career choice," I answered automatically, parroting the words I'd said to myself a thousand times before, echoing my father. "Well, it was supposed to be..."

"Okay," he said slowly, "but..."

"But what?"

"I can't imagine you as an accountant."

"Why not? You think just because I'm blonde with big boobs that I can't be smart, too?"

"Whoa!" he said, his tone surprised. "Where'd that come from? Have I ever treated you like you were dumb?"

"Sorry," I said, at last. "But you wouldn't be the first guy to assume that."

"I know you're smart—I was just wondering why CPA? It seems kind of ... stuffy for you."

"I'll be able to earn good money and then spend my leisure time doing what interests me, hobbies and such."

Cody shook his head. "Jeez! Are you 22 or 52? What's got you so afraid of living?"

"Don't be mean!"

"Ava..."

He put his arm around my shoulders, and hugged me while I rested my head against him.

"If you want to be a CPA, then go for it. It's just that you always look kind of sad when you talk about it ... like it's not what you really want to do."

I studied the pink, jeweled flip-flops that I'd picked out the day before, while I thought about my answer.

"I've always wanted to work in art museums."

I hadn't admitted that to anyone since I was 16.

"Okay?" he said, scrunching up his forehead like he was studying a calculus question. "And you don't because...?"

"My dad said there weren't many good jobs in that field, and that nobody would hire someone as clumsy as me to work in an art museum. He's a CPA so..."

Cody squeezed my shoulder gently. "I get it. You want to please your old man. But it's your life, Ava. Yours to live any way you want."

I sighed. "You make it sound so easy."

"Nothing's easy about living, but it's a helluva lot harder if you're miserable while you do it."

I gave a small smile. "How'd you get to be so wise? You make me feel like I'm the kid."

I felt his fingers drift down my cheek before he brushed a kiss onto the corner of my mouth. I turned to stare at him, leaning closer...

But our moment was interrupted when the border guard waved us on, and the bus lurched into life.

Two minutes later we were in Mexico, and soon we were rattling and bumping along the streets of Tijuana.

"What do you want to do first?" Cody asked, his eyes glowing, lit up from the inside with his own personal stash of happiness. "Beach, town, or bar?"

"Bar? It's only 10.30AM! If you start drinking now you'll be too trashed to do anything else."

He winked at me. "Not seeing a problem with that."

"Ugh. I read online about this place called El Popo. It's a market where all the locals go. We could have a look around and get a soda and something to eat..."

"Food, yeah! I could definitely eat some tacos."

"You're always thinking about your stomach."

"It's not the only thing I'm always thinking about," he shot back, letting his gaze drop to my cleavage.

"Stop being a perv! We're supposed to be friends!"

"You suggested 'friends'. I'm more sort of 'friends ... whatever'."

"You conned me!" I accused, holding a smile behind my frown.

"Yeah, so sue me."

"I'll just leave your sorry ass in Mexico when I go home," I called over my shoulder as I started to walk away.

He shook his head, grinning. "My sorry ass is following your sorry ass wherever you go."

"Uh-uh. This sorry ass travels solo," I sang, shaking my hips a little.

When he didn't answer, I looked behind me and saw Cody's eyes glued to my butt. I should have felt guilty, but I didn't. I felt desired. The line between friendship and something else was becoming increasingly blurred, and I was the one at fault. Cody had made it clear from the start that he was attracted to me.

And I was certainly attracted to him, but he was holding something back. I could feel it, and it made me nervous. It would be too easy to fall for this boy with the big smile and bigger heart.

"Come on," I said, turning to grab his arm. "Let's feed you."

We bought some delicious tacos from a street vendor, then wandered along, hand-in-hand through the market, eyes popping out at the sight of the amazing candies. We bought Sopapilla cheesecake and white coconut alfajores for dessert, and Cody bought candied pineapple, mango, and Chilacayote squash for his mom.

He wanted to buy a bottle of tequila, too, but I thought it

was too early to start hitting the hard stuff. And even though he was 6'2" and fifty pounds heavier than me, I still felt responsible for him.

As we browsed through the market, I found a store that sold local tie-dyed fabrics and went to have a look around. Cody refused to come in on the grounds he still had his man-card, and sauntered off, collecting admiring glances wherever he went.

When I came out 15 minutes later, he was looking very pleased with himself.

"What did you do?" I asked, suspiciously.

"I scored," he said, his face deadpan but his eyes giving away his excitement.

"Wow, that was quick. Poor girl."

His eyes widened for a second, then he laughed.

"Nah, I'm with the prettiest girl in town already," he winked at me, throwing a casual arm around my shoulder. "I got something to, um, enjoy later."

"I'm really hoping you're going to say a bottle tequila, but since I can't see one..."

He shrugged lightly. "Just some loco weed."

I frowned.

"You were really taking a risk—if you'd asked the wrong person or ... it probably isn't the real thing anyway. You've probably bought a bag of herbs."

"Oh, it's herbal, alright," he laughed. "Very medicinal."

"Hmm..."

"Did you know some doctors prescribe it for pain relief?"

"Yes, I had heard that, but it's hardly the case here. Just promise me that you won't try and take any back across the border."

He looked amused and irritated. "I'm not an idiot."

"Remains to be seen," I muttered under my breath.

Cody grabbed my hand and swung our arms together like a couple of kids.

"Don't be mad—I just want to cross some more things off our list."

Nope, definitely couldn't stay mad at him.

We stopped at a liquor store and Cody proudly bought two six-packs of beer. And although he glanced longingly at a bottle of locally brewed tequila, he didn't buy any.

"Enjoying yourself?" I teased, as he tucked the six-packs under his arm with a wide grin.

It wasn't that long since I'd bought my first drink without using fake ID. I remembered how good it felt, how grown up.

Most of the time Cody seemed older than his years, but every now and then, the boy in him came out to play. He had such a thirst for life, such a way of seeing the good in every situation; happiness just poured out of him. I'd genuinely never met anyone like him. He was blessed.

We found our way to a pretty park, not far from the main drag. Wide-leafed palms merged into a thicker canopy of leaves, the further we made our way into the forest behind, as I refused to go anywhere if there was the smallest chance we might be seen. Eventually, we settled ourselves under the secluded shade of a eucalyptus, sitting criss-cross applesauce on the long grass at the base of the tree.

"I feel really conspicuous," I hissed.

Cody shook his head in amusement.

"Seriously!" I whined. "If we get caught we'll go to prison."

He rolled his eyes in disbelief and smirked at me.

"First, no one will see us here—in fact I'm kind of worried they'll only find a bunch of bones a few years down the line, because you route-marched us into the land that time forgot; and second, you can have five grams for personal use—I googled it."

"Yeah? Well, your research sucks, because I googled it, too, and that's only if you're Mexican, and as far as I know, unless you've been lying your ass off, you're from Kansas."

"Oh."

"Yeah. Oh."

"Well, if anyone finds us—which they won't—we'll be able to hear them coming, and I'll drop it on the grass. Grass on grass: no one will find that."

"They'll be able to smell it, doofus!"

"Just wave your hands around. We'll tell them you saw a huge flying cockroach."

I couldn't help laughing.

"Fine! Just do it. Smoke your loco weed. I'm going to have beer."

We kicked off our shoes, enjoying the soft tickle of grass under our bare feet, and opened the beer, Cody sighing with pleasure. It was so peaceful, the sounds of the world far away. Then he reached into his pocket, and I watched, fascinated, as he rolled his smoke with nimble fingers.

"Hey, you've done that before!"

He looked up and smiled. "I didn't say I hadn't."

"But ... it's on your wish list!"

"I've never done it in Tijuana with an ice cold beer and my best friend."

I couldn't help the warm glow of happiness that spread through me as he said that, despite my prim disapproval of what he was doing.

He lit the end, took a long drag, and breathed out slowly, blowing the sweet smoke toward me.

"It'll keep the flying cockroaches away," he said, raising an eyebrow. Then he lay back contentedly, his long legs stretched out, his bare feet crossed at the ankle.

With his eyes closed, hands resting across his stomach, I took the opportunity to drink him in.

His shoulders were broad and strong, and I could see the new tattoo peeping out beneath the sleeve of his white t-shirt. Every time he took another hit of the weed, his biceps bulged and the t-shirt lifted on his ridged stomach. His cheeks were slightly flushed, pink overlaying the golden tan, and his long lashes fanned out as his eyelids fluttered.

"I know you're staring at me," he said. "I can feel you looking at me."

"No, I'm not," I lied.

His full lips curved upward in a lazy smile, but his eyes

remained closed. He took another hit then cracked one eye to look across at me.

"Want to try some? It's good stuff—it'll just give you a nice buzz."

I was about to turn him down when I hesitated. I'd been so scared of failing in college, that I'd hardly ever taken the chance to let my hair down. Math wasn't my strong suit, so I'd had to bust my ass to get decent grades. I studied and I worked: the worst I'd ever done was to get drunk at a couple of frat parties, and sleep with the wrong guys.

I'd never get this chance again; not here like this, with Cody.

"Okay," I said, nervously. "What do I do?"

His lazy smile stretched wider.

"Whatever feels good."

That wasn't at all what I meant, so I ignored the inviting look on his face and plucked the roach from his fingers, inhaling deeply the way he had. Only to have a massive coughing fit as the smoke hit the back of my throat.

Cody sat up quickly, swaying slightly, then passed me some beer to calm the rasping in my throat. He rubbed my shoulders, the movement slowing to gentle strokes, as the concern in his eyes faded.

"Are you okay?"

I nodded slowly, looking up at him. I'd stopped coughing although my eyes were still watering, but the touch of his hands had sparked something else.

We both knew it, but neither of us acknowledged it.

"Yes, I'm fine." And I took another hesitant drag to prove it.

I passed the joint back to him and lay on the grass, mesmerized by the fingers of sunlight that dappled the leaves. I could almost see my hopes and dreams drifting hazily above me, floating nearby but just out of reach.

"My head's buzzing," I sighed. "It feels nice ... sort of like I'm floating in a warm bath ... or drifting like a balloon. I could just float away if someone cut my string."

He lay back next to me and turned his face toward mine, his eyelids heavy over his beautiful eyes.

"That's why it's called a high, pretty girl."

"The colors are so amazing—like a painting, but brighter. We're in our own private art gallery."

I felt his fingers drift down my arm, winding around my wrist until he was holding my hand.

"If you could do anything you wanted, what would you do?"

I sighed, feeling contented but still with an edge of sadness. Why did all the good stuff go by so fast?

"I'd fly to Florence," I began, my voice dreamy and soft. "That's in Italy. I'd spend every day in the Uffizi art gallery. It's the most amazing place, one of the oldest art museums in the world, and it's got paintings by Botticelli, Giotto and Leonardo da Vinci. I'd eat pasta and learn Italian; I'd ride a scooter and live in a building that was hundreds of years old, and I wouldn't be boring old Ava Lawton anymore."

His fingers squeezed mine tightly, then he rolled onto his hip to stare into my eyes.

"There's nothing boring about you, pretty girl."

I snorted loudly and the sound made me giggle.

"Oh come on! Being a CPA is not exactly exciting."

Cody didn't laugh. He continued to stare at me, his expression too serious.

"If you decide to do that, well fine, but you shouldn't give up on you dreams, Ava. Life is too short to live with regrets. You should go to Italy, live your dream. You can always come back and be an accountant. But suppose Italy is just as great as you think it could be?"

I sat up and took a long drink of beer, suddenly feeling very thirsty.

"I don't want to talk about that," I snapped, then regretted my harsh words. My voice softened as I gazed down at my beautiful boy. "Tell me about Cody Richards. What's he really like under there?"

I poked him in his firm chest, and he captured my hand, laying it over his heart.

"He's just a regular guy."

"You glow. You're all glowy."

He laughed softly. "I think that's the loco weed talking."

"No, it's you. That's what you're like. You glow and you're all light. Everyone sees it. You're like sunshine—with a great ass."

Oh wow, the weed really was kicking in.

He laughed happily. "So basically you're saying the sun shines out of my ass?"

"Yes," I said, pleased that he understood.

He took a final drag before stubbing out the smoke and tucking the butt into his jeans' pocket.

"I've never been on an airplane," he said, his voice quiet.

"Really?" My voice was much louder, and I had to concentrate to adjust my volume. "Really? You've never flown anywhere? Not even when you came to San Diego?"

"Nope. We had a U-haul with all our shit in it, so we drove from Junction City in my truck."

"Well, if you've never been in a plane, why do you want to jump out of one?"

My voice sounded like I was complaining, and I could see from the curve of his cheek that he was smiling.

"I want to experience it. It must be cool to be flying above the ground so you're not attached to anything, just traveling through space, like you're completely weightless, like you've got wings."

"It's nothing like that," I insisted. "Traveling by plane means being shoved in a cigar tube with stinky people and praying that you walk away without being dead at the end."

He laughed.

"No way! It's awesome. You start off in one place and you end up somewhere completely different—in a different time zone or an ocean away. It's like magic."

"I love the way you see things," I sighed. "I wish I could be like that."

I snuggled closer to him, so my head was resting on his shoulder, and his arm was wrapped around me.

"You've gotta practice looking for that silver lining, pretty girl."

"It's easier with you," I admitted.

There was a long silence, then he simply said, "Good."

We lay together, talking lazily, finishing the beer, until I realized that the pressure on my bladder was becoming unbearable.

"I have to pee!"

"Yeah, me too."

I sat up, a wave of dizziness making my head spin. Boy, I was hammered. This was going to be interesting.

Cody stood up unsteadily, then staggered off into the gloom, returning a couple of minutes later with a satisfied look on his face.

"I'm not doing *that!*" I hissed. "There could be creepy crawlies and ... and jaguars."

He stifled a laugh.

"I'll watch your back."

"You're not watching anything, mister!"

It was a tough call whether to walk into the forest's sliding shadows, or stagger crab-wise with my legs crossed all the way back into town.

"Okay, I'm going to do it ... but you have to sing to me so I know where you are."

"You want me to what?"

"Just do it, okay! I'm freaked out enough about this."

"Fine. What do you want me to sing? And just so's you know, I don't do show tunes."

"Stop teasing me!"

"How about if I whistle?"

"Whatever."

As I tottered into the trees, I heard his clear, tenor voice singing the Johnny Cash number *Song for the Life*. I paused to listen, the notes rising upward into the twilight, and something tugged at me deep inside. A little warning voice rang in my head, *I could fall for this boy*.

The thought was unnerving, but not as scary as I thought it might be.

He was still singing when I walked back, his voice softer now, almost introspective, and I didn't know if he was singing for me or himself.

"I'm back."

He turned and smiled at me.

"Better now?"

I shook my head slowly.

"What's wrong?" he asked, concerned.

"I want you to kiss me."

His eyes widened, and he took a deep, stuttering breath.

"I thought you wanted to be friends?"

I took a step closer to him, so close I could feel the heat from his body.

"I've changed my mind."

"Ava, I'm not sure this is a good idea..."

"No, it's not; it's a *great* idea."

I wrapped my arms around him, stroking the silky hair at the nape of his neck, gently pulling his head toward mine.

He was hesitant, but not unwilling. I saw desire flaring in his eyes, and his large hands locked around my waist.

Our lips touched, a soft brush, and I felt his body quiver. He kissed me again, more firmly this time, and a strangled growl erupted from his throat. His hands slid to my hips, tightening almost painfully as he pulled my body flush against him.

"Ava," he whispered, but whatever words he was going to say were silenced when my tongue flicked across his lower lip.

He moaned softly, and my tongue slipped into his mouth.

His body trembled, then he kissed me back, his tongue stroking against mine, teasing, tasting, whispering across my lips.

His hands began to move, one sliding down to cup the curve of my butt, one moving up my spine, leaving a burning trail of want.

Desire like I'd never known surged through my body. I'd

never kissed my best friend before either, but this was the gold standard of kisses; everything else would be measured against it.

His mouth kissed along the line of my jaw, sucking gently at the pulse point on my neck, before moving lower, the cool fire of his touch igniting my body.

My own hands were roaming over his body, under his t-shirt, stroking the warm, silky skin, dipping down to the low waistband of his jeans, my thumbs grazing over his hipbones.

His confident kisses stuttered, and he groaned deeply.

The erection that had been hinted at this morning was now pressing into my stomach, promising insane pleasure to come. By now, his body was trembling uncontrollably, and I could tell he was within a few seconds of losing it.

Then he clamped his hands around my wrists, halting their inquisitive journey.

"Ava, we can't," he breathed. "I don't have anything ... I didn't think..."

"There are other things we can do," I said, pushing up his t-shirt and laying wet kisses across his chest.

"I want to, believe me I want to," he gasped, "but not when you're drunk, not when you're high."

"Aren't you the one who told me to take a chance?"

"Yes, but..."

We heard the sound of voices at the same time.

It seemed we weren't the only people who'd sought out the seclusion of the most remote part of the public park.

At least four men, all talking rapidly in Spanish.

I suddenly felt unnerved and vulnerable in the listening forest.

Cody lowered his lips to my ear and spoke softly.

"We're going to walk away quietly. It'll be okay."

He took my hand, and we moved silently through the trees, until the open space of the park spread out in front of us.

Near panic turned to breathless giggling, and Cody grinned as he pulled me across a gravel path in a slow jog, my flip-flops tripping me several times.

Back on Avenida Revolucion, we felt safer, despite the raucous nightlife that was beginning to emerge.

"I definitely need a drink after that," I said, slightly breathless.

"Take your pick," said Cody, sweeping his arm toward the street full of bars.

We strolled hand-in-hand, ignoring the places that were too packed or too noisy, finally stopping at a small, trendy-looking bar called Mandra.

A waiter was serving a table of American girls with colorful cocktails, piled high with fruit and those cute little umbrellas.

Which gave me an idea.

I pushed Cody into an empty table and marched up to the bar, returning a minute later with two ridiculous, comedy cocktails.

"What did you do?" he laughed, poking at a piece of fresh pineapple.

"Don't mock," I said, solemnly. "I got this for you specially."

His laughter softened to a beautiful smile.

"I'm sure I'll love it," he said, "but you'll have to tell me what the hell is in it."

I gave him a superior smile.

"Vodka, peach schnapps, creme de cassis, and orange and cranberry juice. It's called 'Sex on the Beach'."

Cody laughed again, until I put the straw between my lips and sucked hard. His gaze darkened, and I saw his Adam's apple bob up and down as he swallowed several times, before gulping down his drink in one go.

The taste was sharp and too sweet but delicious ... and potent as I stood on tottering legs to go to the bathroom an hour later.

When I returned, I could tell Cody was well on his way to being hammered too, because he spent a pleasant half-hour kissing and sucking my neck, and playing with my hair. I didn't stop him.

Too soon it was time to go if we wanted to catch the last

bus back to San Diego. Grabbing some tacos from a street vendor, we headed to the bus station, and back to our real lives.

During the long wait at the border, my buzz began to fade away, leaving me mellow and sleepy. I didn't know whether to be pleased or disappointed that our evening had been interrupted, but there was no awkwardness between us. I leaned against Cody's firm shoulder, our fingers twined together.

"You have leaves in your hair, pretty girl."

I opened my eyes to look at him, secretly loving that he called me 'pretty'.

"And we crossed two things off the list."

His lips moved, then turned into a warm smile, but he didn't reply.

I wanted to ask him to come back to my place and spend the night, but I bit back the words and said something else entirely.

"Thank you for today, Cody. It's been another first for me."

He smiled. "Me, too."

It was only later that I wondered what he meant by that.

CHAPTER SIX

TWO DAYS LATER, CODY CALLED ME AT AN UNGODLY HOUR, ordering me to be ready in 20 minutes. He didn't tell me what we were doing, just that I should wear jeans and comfortable shoes.

He'd interrupted a particularly good dream where his lips were doing more than they'd done in Mexico, so I wasn't very happy. But then again, real Cody was preferable to dream Cody, even if dream Cody was taking liberties with my body that the real one seemed reluctant to explore.

Damn, this was getting confusing.

I wobbled sleepily down the stairs and out of the apartment as soon as I heard his truck.

He kissed me quickly and quirked an eyebrow when I muttered something about "Dream Cody being a better kisser."

"Are you actually awake, pretty girl?" he asked.

I grunted something and leaned back in my seat, wondering who'd glued lead weights to my eyelids.

I was surprised that Cody didn't stop at Muffin Heaven, instead heading to a part of town that was unfamiliar. He finally pulled up outside a rundown building decorated with a cheerful sign announcing we'd arrived at 'The Bridge'.

"Come on," he said, tugging on my hand. "We've got to help set up breakfast."

"What is this place?"

"It's a homeless shelter where I've been volunteering," he said, nonchalantly.

I sat up, suddenly wide awake.

"Really? Wow! How long have you been coming here?"

"A few weeks," he said. "Two days after we wrote our wish list."

"You didn't say anything!"

"I wanted it to be a surprise, but I needed to make sure you'd be safe here first. Some of the shelters are men only, and I wasn't going to risk my pretty girl around a bunch of guys."

I smiled when he called me *his* pretty girl. I didn't mind that at all.

"But this place," he continued, "it helps families that are in transition. After breakfast, there's a food and clothing distribution—all stuff that's been donated."

I leaned over and kissed him firmly.

"You are so *good*," I said.

He smiled and raised his eyebrows. "I can be bad, too."

God, I hoped that was true, but I was very aware that we were in public, and getting more than our share of curious stares from a line of people waiting outside for breakfast to be served.

"Hold that thought, mister, we've got work to do."

Cody took me inside and introduced me to some of the other volunteers. At least I think he did—the introduction was all one way as everyone seemed to recognize my name, and smiled knowingly.

There wasn't time to make small talk because we were whisked into the kitchen, and I was put to work making a stack of pancakes.

Cody was a blur of activity: filling beakers with juice, cutting up slices of melon, and grilling dozens and dozens of pieces of bacon.

People started lining up as soon as the doors opened at

7AM sharp. Cody was at the serving window, a smile and a word for everybody. I watched him from the corner of my eye, impressed by how at ease he seemed. Then I began to sweat as my stack of pancakes reduced rapidly and I quickly whisked some more flour, milk and eggs.

When the line finally began to shrink, the volunteers were allowed to take a plate of food and sit at the long benches to eat with the customers.

I filled up two plates for us, and Cody carried the juice in plastic cups, leading us to a seat where a dad was sitting with his two sons.

They'd been chatting to Cody earlier, but with me they were shy. Eventually, he got the kids to relax by promising to play a game of basketball after, and then there was no shutting them up. They asked him about living in Kansas, and why he'd come to San Diego, and what he thought of the ocean, and a hundred more questions that I'd been longing to ask. He answered everything, but there were times when he deliberately turned the conversation away from topics he found uncomfortable. For someone who seemed so open, he was still an enigma.

"Is she your girlfriend?" Kevin asked, pointing at me with his spoon.

Cody looked at me and winked.

"Pretty, isn't she?"

Kevin scowled and stuffed his mouth with more melon.

"Girls suck," he mumbled.

Cody leaned over and whispered in my ear, "Is that true?"

If my face flushed any redder, they could have used me as a traffic light.

I punched his arm as he laughed.

I only realized later that he hadn't answered Kevin's question. I guess that meant I *wasn't* his girlfriend; just a friend who was a girl. A girl he'd kissed in Mexico. When he was high. And drunk.

I had to remember that, because seeing him here had made me fall a little bit in love with him. Or a lot.

After we'd helped clear away the breakfast things, I was put on dish-washing duty. Cody was at the front, helping with the food and clothes distribution. I was amazed and humbled by the number of people coming to the old building for help.

Some looked like they were street people, but most just looked ordinary, the Recession having hit everywhere. Each one had a heart-breaking story of lost jobs that led to debt, or bad choices that led to them losing their homes.

There were also a number of vets, the youngest being just 24 years old. His name was Jason and he hadn't been able to settle after he'd finished two tours in Afghanistan. His parents hadn't wanted him back either, and he'd ended up living in various shelters across the city.

He introduced me to his friends, Wayne and Arthur, who were grizzled Vietnam veterans, and flirted with me shamelessly.

Their stories were similar and equally sad: changed by what they'd seen, changed by war, unable to cope with their old lives, broken marriages, children who didn't want to know them anymore.

Jason was still optimistic that there was more out there for him, if he could just get himself back on his feet. Wayne and Arthur had the resigned weariness of the long-term homeless, living with the tedium of each day being the same: a hunt for food and somewhere to sleep, basic things that I'd always taken for granted.

I could see why Cody had wanted to add this to our wish list, although I wondered if it was more for my benefit than his; he already seemed to know that each day was precious, and that each new day was the road untaken.

After the food distribution, Jason joined Cody in starting a game of pickup basketball for the kids.

Alli, one of the organizers came to bring me a cup of coffee while we watched the guys running around and yelling happily.

"It's been so wonderful having Cody here; he's such a breath of fresh air. We're all going to miss him when he leaves at the end of August."

"Excuse me? When he leaves?"

Her eyes widened and she stammered and stuttered her way through a reply.

"Oh, I thought ... isn't he? Oh, I probably got that wrong."

But I didn't miss the look of pity that she shot me before turning to talk to another volunteer.

Maybe Cody was going away for college, or maybe he just didn't think he'd have time to volunteer once he was back in school. That would make sense. But I was hurt that he hadn't said anything to me—he'd always been irritatingly vague when I asked about his plans for the fall.

I was quiet when I climbed back into his truck an hour later. I think he assumed it was because the shelter had given me food for thought, because he talked about how grateful he was to have a roof over his head and his mom in his life.

The shelter and the people I'd met had definitely affected me, but it was Alli's parting comment that was making my brain work overtime.

I thought I'd give Cody the benefit of the doubt before I accused him of anything.

"Jason seemed really nice," I began.

"Yeah, he's great. I was talking to him about maybe taking a class in carpentry. He doesn't want an indoor job—I can relate to that."

"What about you? Will you be taking any classes in the fall?"

"Life is one big lesson," he said with a small smile.

"So, no firm plans?"

He looked at me sideways.

"Not really."

"It's just that Alli said you were leaving at the end of August; that sounded like a pretty firm plan."

He shrugged.

"It's easier for them to work out volunteer rosters if they know who's going to be around. I just wanted to let them know which days I could help this summer."

I was about to argue when he changed the subject again.

"Okay, so I've got something lined up for this afternoon, but you don't have to do it if you don't want."

"If I don't want to what?"

He slid his eyes across to me before staring back at the road.

"Jumping out of an airplane."

The blood drained from my face, and if I hadn't been sitting down, I'd have fainted.

"You ... you didn't!"

"Um, yeah, I kind of did. But no one's going to make you— do it if *you* want to."

"I think I've been pretty clear about my thoughts on the sanity of someone who'd do something like that."

He grinned.

"Seriously, Cody! Do you have a death wish or something?"

His eyes widened, but then he shook his head.

"It'll be fun. And you don't do it by yourself; it's a tandem jump, so you'll be harnessed to an instructor. You don't even have to open your eyes. Just see how you feel when you get there."

Which was why, half an hour later, a burly man called Cesar was strapped inappropriately close against my back, and I was wearing goggles that made me look like Millhouse from *The Simpsons*.

Cody was vibrating with excitement, and even signing a waiver that promised we wouldn't sue in the event of death didn't deter him.

I was hyperventilating as we were seated awkwardly in the small mono-winged plane. He held my hand as we took off, rubbing my fingers and telling me how awesome it was going to be, until I wanted to scream or slap him.

The plane circled slowly, rising steadily upward. I squeezed my eyes shut, ignoring his enthusiastic commentary that told me he could see Mexico.

Cody was jumping first. I heard him begging his instructor, Ralph, to do a forward flip out of the plane. I thought there was every chance that I'd vomit just watching him.

When we finally reached jump altitude, Cody shuffled to the exit, moving crabwise with Ralph close behind. The pilot cut the propeller, and for the briefest moment, the only sound was the rush of wind over the wings.

"Three, two, one, exit!" yelled Ralph, and Cody leapt forward, somersaulting out of the plane. I screamed and Cesar laughed.

I peered out of the scratched plastic window, seeing two figures hurtling below, already tiny and nearly out of sight.

A short prayer fluttered in my throat, but not for me—for that crazy boy, falling through the air.

The engine cut back in, and we circled higher again. Then it was my turn. I was sweating, almost crying, and Cesar had to jump with my body hanging limp in front of him.

The plane spiraled away, or maybe it was us spiraling. Cesar tapped on my shoulder to make me open my eyes, so the photographer who jumped with us could get my picture. But as soon as I pried my eyes open, the view and the furious air took my breath away.

Downtown San Diego was spread out below, and the Pacific glittered and glowed, sparkling as the sun hit the shifting water. I could see Coronado, Chula Vista and the red earth of the border with Mexico, so close I felt I could reach out and touch it.

I was falling through the sky at billions of miles an hour, my hair streaming behind me and my skin rippling, yet it felt like I was floating. It was the strangest feeling.

I forgot to scream, and gave the biggest smile at the camera.

Cesar tapped on my shoulder again, telling me to put my arms at my side and keep my body rigid like we'd practiced. Suddenly we were flying forward, and if I sprouted wings I couldn't have been more surprised.

I was flying, I was free, and truthfully, I'd never been happier.

Cesar pulled the chute at last, and instead of the ground

rushing toward us, we floated back to earth, rocking gently under the colorful canopy.

Cody was waiting for me, and as soon as I was out of harness, he sprinted across, sweeping me up so my feet left the ground again. The almost brutal kiss he gave me was as dizzying as jumping out of an airplane from 13,000 feet. And just like that leap of faith, I felt my heart pounding in my chest.

The other men gave a ribald cheer as Cody kissed me soundly, again and again, until his lips slowly gentled against mine.

"Wow," I said, and I didn't know if I was talking about the parachute jump or the kiss.

Probably the kiss.

CHAPTER SEVEN

I didn't see Cody for nearly a week after our visit to the Bridge shelter and the whole crazy business of throwing ourselves out of an airplane.

And that kiss. That short, sweet, punishing kiss—a kiss that I couldn't stop thinking about. Adrenaline, that's what it was, damn it.

I'd been offered extra shifts at the coffee shop, and I couldn't say no to the handful of tips, or the small but regular wage.

Worse still, given how confused I was about my feelings for Cody and life in general, my family found out that I'd lost my job at Wallman & Wallman. Chloe phoned there to speak to me. It was my own damn fault—I'd been ignoring her texts and calls on my cell phone, so I should have known that she wouldn't just let it lie.

I confessed to her what James Wallman had said and done, and I must admit I got a big smile out of her desire to fly over and 'kick his balls through his teeth'. But then she'd gone and screwed up my appreciation by stating that she'd made a reservation for me on the first flight home. Well, back to Fayetteville, or, if you were an army brat like the kids I went to school with Fayettenam, North Carolina—the place the rest of my family called home.

She'd been stunned when I refused to even consider it, then angry, then disbelieving, then angry again. It had been an exhausting conversation. She threatened to fly out to San Diego and drag me home. I told her that I wasn't going. She told Dad, and he threatened to fly out to San Diego and drag me home.

When that didn't work and I reminded him that I was an adult, he told me not to be such a child. Then he refused to help me make the rent on my very expensive apartment that *he* had made me get because it had underground parking and good security.

Well, fine. If he was cutting me off, I was cutting him off. I ended the call and contacted the rental agent to give notice. I had a month to find somewhere else to live. Oh, and get a job that paid reasonable money so I could afford another apartment. Easy.

Cody had been busy, too. I assumed it was something to do with the shelter, but he gave vague answers when I asked him, admitting only that he had 'stuff' to do and that he was 'working on the wish list'.

We kept in touch with texts and late night phone calls that often meandered through to the next morning, but when I told him what had happened with my dad, he insisted on seeing me straight away.

We met at the park during my lunch break, so he could throw a tennis ball for Oscar at the same time. As soon as he saw me, his delighted grin made me feel everything would be okay; just for a second I could believe that I had no problems.

He reached out and pulled me into a tight hug, and we stood there holding each other, enjoying the warmth that came from another person's body, and from the simple fact that he cared.

Oscar lollopped toward me, pushing his heavy head against my thigh, looking for his share of affection. I scratched his ears and buried my hands in his thick fur while he sighed contentedly.

"I think I'm jealous," said Cody, laughing lightly.

"Well, he is darn good looking with great hair," I teased.

"Now I'm hurt, too."

I grinned and looked up at him, then frowned slightly.

"You look tired."

His eyes flickered away from mine and he gripped the back of his neck with one hand.

"Late night. Did you call your dad back yet?"

"No, and I'm not going to. Not yet. If he thinks he can bully me into going back to Fayetteville, he's very wrong."

"That's my girl," said Cody, wrapping his arm around my shoulder and pulling me toward him.

Am I? I wondered. *Am I your girl?* But I didn't say the words.

We talked for half an hour and he bought me another frozen yogurt that I shared with Oscar. Not that we took turns, or anything gross like that, but when I'd eaten about half of it, I tossed the rest to him and he slurped it down happily.

Cody told me how Kevin and his family were getting on at the shelter, and that Jason had even started applying for carpentry courses and apprenticeships.

We talked about my dad and sisters, about where I grew up, and about college. Everything I said fascinated him, and I soaked up every drop of attention he had to give.

We also talked about how we could make the Monument Valley trip happen. It wasn't something we could just wing, so it needed to be planned. I was really excited about it, even though I'd never ridden a horse. Cody said he'd ridden once or twice when he was a kid, but had given it up before high school. At least he wasn't a complete novice.

I wasn't sure I could afford the trip, or even take the time off work, given my precarious financial situation, but Cody just smiled and reminded me that it was one of his wishes and that he wanted pay for it. Then he said, "Do what you need to, Ava, but don't let life be something that happens while you're looking in the other direction."

I was still thinking about that when he kissed me on the top of my head, and said he had to get Oscar home.

I watched him walk away. He looked like he was talking to Oscar because every now and then, the dog's shaggy head would look up at him, tongue lolling to the side. Cody turned once and seemed surprised to see me watching him. He grinned and waved, then carried on walking away.

I watched until they were out of sight, then hurried back to work alone, wondering why he hadn't kissed me like he did in Tijuana.

I'd replayed our kisses over and over, telling myself it couldn't possibly have been as amazing as I remembered. It was *just* a kiss; it must have been the marijuana; it must have been the adrenaline rush of surviving falling out of an airplane.

Or maybe it was just wishful thinking.

But then he messaged me an hour later, telling me to keep Friday and Saturday clear, saying that he'd pick me up at 6AM, to dress for the desert and to bring a sweater.

We were really going to do this—we were going to ride through Monument Valley and sleep under the stars. It was sad to think that almost everything on Cody's wish list would now be done. Maybe he'd write another one—maybe we could write one together again. And maybe this time I'd put 'travel to Italy' on my list.

I'd been thinking about that more often lately. When I was 16 and still believed that dreams came true, I spent a lot of time researching what I needed to do to get to Florence. It was surprisingly straightforward to apply for a work-study visa, and I wondered how much the rules might have changed in the last eight years. Definitely something for me to look into; maybe something that I could do more than just dream about. Maybe.

I'd worked a late shift the night before our next adventure, so I was tired, and a little grumpy. I would have loved the opportunity to sleep in, but I was really excited to see Cody, too. We were going to have a whole weekend together—and I was going to find out how he really felt about us, even if it killed me.

The rumble of his truck pulled me out of my musings, and

I thumped down the stairs, my small overnight bag bumping against my hip.

He met me at the door, but his face was so serious and stern, that I was a little intimidated.

My mouth opened to speak, but no words came out. Cody was staring at me, his gaze flicking between my chest and my mouth.

Cody my friend was gone, replaced by a man whose eyes demanded more. He took two paces, then pinned me to the wall outside the apartment building, searing my lips with a kiss that seemed desperate, as if all the kisses in the world were about to run out.

It was so different from the gentle peck he'd given me when we last met in the park. My head was spinning.

I fisted my hands into the front of his t-shirt and pulled him even closer, pressing my lips against his, touching him and tasting him and feeling the weight of his body as he leaned into me.

My hands gripped his t-shirt still tighter and I felt his fingers rubbing circles on the bare skin above my waistband. I was superheating, a few short steps from exploding. And if I did, I was taking him with me. Or in me. One way or another, I was *not* letting this man go without a fight.

Finally, he pulled away, panting slightly, his cheeks flushed and his eyes dark with want.

"Is that how you say 'Good morning' in Kansas?" I asked, breathlessly.

He shook his head, his mouth solemn, although his eyes danced with naked joy.

"Nope, that's a San Diego wake-up call."

"It could catch on," I smiled weakly, my whole body on fire.

He stared down at me, letting his eyes take in every part of my body, wholly unapologetic for once. It was like being undressed by the sheer power of his mind. I flushed again, and was about to drag him upstairs.

But then he sighed, and tugged his eyes away from me.

"Sorry I attacked you. I've wanted to do that for a while."

"I'm not sorry. I've wanted you to do that, too. In fact, I'd decided that if you didn't, I would."

The surprise and pleasure on his face made me blush and giggle. God! I hated that. I was *not* the giggling type. Until I was. Aw, shoot.

I huffed out quietly and Cody took a deep breath, before towing me toward his truck.

"Big day, pretty girl. Beginning with breakfast."

I let him help me into the truck, then leaned back in my seat, warmed by his possessive touch, stomach rumbling quietly.

He smiled, and placed another a quick kiss on my lips before starting the truck's engine. Except this time he held my hand, letting go only to use the turn signal, then immediately taking hold of my fingers again.

We stopped an hour outside the city to load up on breakfast foods. Well, I did; Cody said he wasn't hungry, but watched with amusement as I stuffed myself with bacon, eggs and pancakes.

It was a 10 hour drive to Monument Valley so Cody had reluctantly agreed to let me do my share behind the wheel.

Very reluctantly.

He wouldn't take his eyes off me the entire time.

"I'm not going to crash your truck," I said, testily. "I *do* know how to drive. I've been driving longer that you, Mr. Only-18."

"I can't help it," he said. "It's kinda hot seeing you driving my truck."

He laughed as I flushed again. He seemed to enjoy getting me all wound up. He'd pay for that later; I'd make sure of it.

We had lunch at a truck stop forty miles north of Phoenix, but Cody left most of his burritos, saying they were too spicy. I tried to give him some of my tuna sub instead, but he waved me off saying he liked to watch me eat. Yeah, that wasn't going to make me feel self-conscious *at all*.

I slept for a couple of hours in the afternoon as we headed steadily north, and when I woke, we were only fifty miles from the Utah border. Well, that's not entirely the truth. I woke up, but stayed with my eyes closed as I took the time to really consider what I was doing here and how this amazing boy—man—had turned my life around to the point where everything I thought I believed in suddenly seemed wrong, or out-dated.

He'd come to mean so much to me, but he was holding himself back and I didn't know why. I didn't understand how one minute he could kiss me like he needed my air to breathe, and the next he treated me like I was his little sister or something.

He wanted me to be part of his wish-list—hell, it even had a couple of my wishes on it, including the one about spending the night under the stars. And I'd seen the sleeping bags in the back of his truck before we left San Diego.

Which was something else we hadn't discussed. Sleeping.

Or not sleeping, which bothered me more.

"I know you're awake."

His voice made me sit up guiltily.

"No, I wasn't."

His laugh was silky and his beautiful lips quirked upward.

"You snore when you're asleep."

"I do not!"

"You sound like a groundhog or something, all these cute little snuffling sounds."

"You're so mean!"

"And your mouth drops open, so you probably drool, too."

"Stop it!"

"So, as you haven't been doing any of those things for the twenty minutes, it makes me wonder what you've been thinking about over there."

Busted.

Well, okay, he brought it up.

"I was thinking about you. I was thinking about us. Is there an 'us'?"

His smile dropped away, but he reached across to hold my hand.

"You're my best friend."

His answer was painful. But it was also evasive.

"I know. You told me that, but is that all? Because you've kissed me three times now and those definitely weren't 'best friend' kisses."

He clenched his teeth together and I could see a muscle tick in his jaw.

"I'm sorry. I shouldn't have done that."

"Don't!" I snapped. "Don't tell me you're sorry for kissing me. It *hurts* me, Cody."

He flinched, and I watched as he gripped the steering wheel more tightly, his knuckles whitening against his tan.

"God, I'm sorry, Ava. You're the last person I'd want to hurt. Ever."

I could hear the sincerity in his voice, but it wasn't enough. I wanted to know where I stood, once and for all.

"When we first met, you tried to ask me out on a date. Do you still want to date me, Cody?"

His reply was forced out between gritted teeth.

"I want to, but I *can't*."

"Stop playing games with me!" I yelled.

He pounded the steering wheel in frustration and yanked it so hard that we skidded off the road and were bouncing along rough ground.

I was a little scared. I'd seen so many different sides to him: happy, sad, serious, playful—but angry Cody was something else.

His eyes flashed and his nostrils flared. He stared straight ahead, fists clenched.

I unclipped my seatbelt hurriedly and held onto the door handle, ready to bolt—even though we were at the side of the road in the middle of pretty much nowhere.

His head turned slowly and he looked at me. His gaze softened and remorse settled across his expressive face.

"Ava..." He cleared his throat and tried again.

"Ava, I want nothing more on this whole earth than to be with you, to tell everyone that I'm yours and you're mine. Hell, I would have tattooed your name across my heart that first day

I met you, but I'm … going away soon. And it's not fair for me to start anything."

"Why is it just your decision? Don't I get any say in this? People go away to school all the time and they stay in touch. I know airplane tickets are expensive and we wouldn't see each other that often, but we could email and write, maybe video chat."

I grew increasingly desperate as he shook his head at each suggestion.

"Wherever you're going, I'll wait for you."

"No!" he shouted. "I don't want you to wait for me! I don't want you to spend your life waiting!"

"You are such a hypocrite!" I yelled, glaring at him, anger boiling out of me. "You want to date me, then you don't. You want to kiss me, then you don't. What are *you* waiting for?"

For a millisecond, he froze in shock, but then we were both moving and our bodies collided together. His arms were around me, crushing my ribs, his teeth scraping across my lips. Then his tongue was in my mouth, hot and hard and demanding, and my hands were under his t-shirt, gouging long lines down his spine. He hissed, and his back arched, giving me space to run my lips and tongue over his chest, teasing and biting his small, masculine nipples.

I felt his hands slide down to my waist, gripping tightly. Then his left hand crept upward, stroking the skin across my ribs, his thumb brushing the underside of my breast. A long, low growl vibrated in his throat as I bit a little harder than I intended, and his fingers caught over the front of my bra.

My hands dropped to his jeans, and I was tugging at the buckle of his belt, feeling the heat pulsing along his thick shaft, when a horn shrieked loudly in our ears, and the truck shook as a sixteen-wheeler barreled past.

I fell back into my seat, embarrassed that I'd been about to mount him in full public view.

"Shit!" Cody rubbed his hands over his face, and dropped his head back.

"Yeah," I said, putting my four years' of college vocabulary to good use.

He gave a dry, humorless chuckle. "I can never catch a fuckin' break."

"Oh, I don't know," I joked. "I think your luck could be changing."

He didn't laugh and the bleak look he gave, curled me up inside.

"I guess we'd better get on the road," he sighed.

I nodded stiffly, and he waited until I'd clipped my seatbelt back into position before bumping back onto the highway.

He didn't speak; instead he reached over to grip my hand.

His fingers were warm and rough and loving around mine, so why did I feel like crying?

"I'm sorry," he whispered.

"I'm tired of you being sorry," I said, pulling my hand free from his.

We drove in silence, but as the final miles passed, the beauty of the world beyond the window pulled me from my angry, frustrated thoughts.

The red earth and blue sky stretched in seemingly endless vibrancy toward the horizon, thick dust coating the road, and flying up in plumes behind our tires. Spires of ancient rock formations grew from the ground, pointing toward the sun that was sinking in the west. Long fingers of shadows crept toward us, and a feeling of peace settled inside me.

I took a deep breath and looked across to Cody. His broad hands were still gripping the steering wheel for dear life, but it was the unshed tears glistening in his eyes that made my heart clench.

And I was struck with a profound truth: it wasn't his own heart that he was trying to protect, it was mine.

I reached over to touch his arm. His eyes flickered to my hand before focusing on the road again. But now a small smiled softened the hard lines of his clenched jaw.

"It's going to be a great weekend," I said, quietly. "Thank you for bringing me."

He nodded and swallowed several times, but he didn't speak. I didn't think he could, so I just rested my hand on his thigh and let him drive in silence.

We arrived at the campsite fifty minutes later, hungry and tired, but without the ragged frustration that had dogged us.

As I opened the door, leaving the air-conditioned cab behind, the heat was almost a living, fire-breathing entity, pounding the ground, and burning the air so it smelled like dry parchment.

Cody took my hand as he lifted me from the truck, and we held each other loosely.

I decided to live in the moment and enjoy the simple pleasure of being held, nuzzling against Cody's firm chest, his arms around me. He dropped soft kisses into my hair, and this time I felt loved and wanted, rather than pushed away and rejected.

I stood on tiptoe to kiss him lightly on the lips and he smiled his beautiful smile.

"Guess we'd better find out where we're sleeping tonight, pretty girl."

"As long as it's with you, I don't care," I replied, boldly.

A faint blush highlighted the sharpness of cheekbones, and he ducked his head.

Chuckling quietly, I squeezed his waist.

"I didn't mean *that*," I said, although maybe I did.

The campsite had a small shop selling Native American artifacts. I looked longingly at the pretty woven mats in a range of broad geometric patterns and earthy tones. But they were beyond my meager budget, so I settled for a pair of dreamcatchers decorated with the image of a wolf, buying one each for me and Cody. It said the wolf was a symbol of protection—I liked that.

When I looked up to find him, he was laughing with the sales assistant as he tried on a range of different Stetsons.

She was definitely flirting with him, although I couldn't blame her—he did look awfully fine in his navy t-shirt and washed-out blue jeans.

"Hey, Ava! You should get one of these!" he grinned, donning a wide, black Stetson. "You'd look awesome!"

The sales assistant had the grace to withhold the scowl she clearly wanted to unleash, and politely handed me a hat to try on.

"Oh, thanks, but I can't afford one," I said, quickly.

"Sure you can. My treat."

"No, Cody. You've paid for everything else; I'm not letting you buy this, too."

"Please," he begged, his eyes urging me not to fight him. "I've never bought a gift for a girl before. Let me do this for you."

How could I argue with that?

I tried to pick one of the cheaper, straw hats, but of course Cody wouldn't hear of it. I ended up with a very pretty dove gray Stetson that I instantly adored. Cody looked pleased with himself, too, and it was worth giving in, just to see that look on his face.

We stocked up with bottles of water and some cereal bars. I really wanted candy, but I knew it would be liquid within minutes. Although the temperature was dropping the closer we got to sunset, it was still in the high nineties.

By the time we came outside to meet our guide, three other couples were also waiting. I was a little disappointed that we'd be with other people as it meant the chances of *sleeping* with Cody instead of just sleeping, were remote.

Well, I could wait. Not for much longer, though.

We introduced ourselves and the others seemed friendly, although more my dad's age than ours. I felt a pulse of annoyance as I remembered how my father had spoken to me. But I recognized that it was also my own fault for letting him treat me as a little girl for so long. My fingers automatically reached for Cody's hand, and he grinned down at me putting his arm around my shoulders before deciding it was too warm for that, instead settling for playing with my hair.

From behind a curve in the rust red road, two jeeps bumped and jolted toward us, skidding to a stop in an impressive cloud of dust. The man who was clearly going to be our tour guide jumped out. His face was the color and texture of an old saddle, but his black eyes sparkled with amusement as we coughed and spluttered.

"Howdy, folks. I'm Joe and I'll be taking y'all out to Big Hogan for sunset. We'll pick up the horses in the morning. Load up your stuff; we'll be heading out in just a minute."

Cody took charge of the sleeping bags and our two backpacks, while I carried the water and goodies that we'd bought.

Then, proudly wearing our new Stetsons, we settled into the back seat of one of the jeeps.

We zoomed off in another dust cloud, bouncing uncomfortably on the hard seats. I gripped hold of Cody and he grinned back at me, joy flashing in his blue eyes.

The jeep rattled across the valley floor, traveling further and further into the past. I peered over my shoulder and was shocked to see a giant red cloud following behind us.

"Sandstorm," shouted Joe, his voice hoarse over the noise of the engine. "But we'll miss it, so don't worry."

Cody tucked his arm around me protectively and I tried to ignore the sudden large drops of rain that spattered the jeep's windows as the temperature dropped rapidly. I shivered and Cody pulled me more tightly against him, as if his body alone could protect me from the whole world. Maybe he could.

The edge of the storm touched us briefly, before speeding off into the growing darkness of the east. After a few more minutes, Joe mashed the brakes and we screeched to a halt against the wall of one of the towering monuments that the valley was named for. As we climbed out of the jeeps, the air seemed suddenly still.

Joe began to speak, his gravelly voice carrying clearly, heavy with the weight of his words.

"My people, the Navajo, call this land Tsebii'nidzisgai; it means 'the valley within the rocks'. It is sacred to us and we lived here many hundred years, and before us, the lost tribe of the Anasazi. We do not know why they left. The old ones say they were summoned to the spirit world. Whatever you believe, you can feel the bones of the world beneath your feet, and the spirits above you in the wide sky. I feel their presence; you must make up your own minds."

I could see Cody was captivated by the words, and even my normal cynicism was swept away in the vast landscape that made a mockery of the length of a human life.

As Joe led us forward on foot, my fingers scraped against the monument, taking in the ancient carvings of animals— buffalo and deer and horses. Always horses. The questions rolled in: who and when and why?

Cody and I broke away from the others, wandering as if hypnotized, until we scrambled through a gap in the rocks, and found ourselves standing inside an enormous cavern, a natural amphitheatre carved out of the sandstone. Slanted light pooled down from a hole at the top in the shape of a massive eye, lines radiating from it like eyelashes, but really stained by the action of wind and rain.

"We call this 'the eye to the heavens'," said Joe, smiling when he saw us jump at his sudden presence.

"It's amazing," Cody breathed, staring upward. "Sort of reassuring—like ... I don't know. Like everything has been seen, or *is* seen."

Joe gazed at him appraisingly. "You are looking for answers."

Cody was surprised by his words, but didn't disagree. Something passed between them, and I watched, puzzled.

"You must meet Grandma Yatzi," said Joe. "She is very old, very wise. The medicine is strong within her—she knows many things."

Cody's eyes brightened.

"Really? Wow! I tried to meet with a medicine man, but I couldn't set anything up for this weekend. So, yeah! Definitely!"

Joe nodded, and drifted away as silently as he'd come.

"We'll finish the list tomorrow," I said, sadly.

Cody didn't speak, but we hugged each other tightly. His

soft lips met mine, and our kiss was just a whisper, a promise that the breeze tugged away.

The jeep's horn sounded at the exact same time my stomach rumbled.

Cody laughed gently. "I can take a hint."

But there was one more stop before supper. Joe drove up to a small platform with a red bluff behind us.

And there we saw the sunset.

My mouth dropped open as a blaze of red and orange burned the sky, setting the mesa alight in an astonishing display of nature or God or some deity more powerful, older, more mesmerizing than anything I had seen.

I think I gasped, and clutched Cody's arm, our silence more meaningful than any words could have been. A deep stillness filled me as I watched the cycle of day to night, as the earth turned. And I was part of it; together we were part of it. My problems seemed small and ridiculous and I promised myself that this was where my life started again: this day, this moment, with this man at my side—if he'd have me.

Darkness bloomed across the sky, and a thousand million stars twinkled seductively. I thought of my mother. She would have liked Cody. I wished I could share this moment with her.

Maybe I was.

CHAPTER EIGHT

Joe drove us back to the site near Big Hogan, the giant eye, and Cody and I watched lazily as the others fussed around pitching tents.

Our plan was much simpler: we'd sleep on the thick, soft sand at the base of the monument, and in the unlikely event of rain, or the slightly more likely event of another sandstorm, we'd sleep in the jeep. It would be a squeeze, but still preferable to a flimsy tent that blocked out the stars.

Cody hollowed out a space in the sand, so we'd be cocooned against the night, womb-like in Mother Earth's belly. Or maybe it would just keep out the cool breeze.

A stray dog trotted over, its skinny frame at odds with its passive friendliness. The others were wary of it, muttering to themselves about the dangers of treating a dog bite all the way out here. Cody smiled when the stray slumped down at his feet, allowing him to stroke its dusty fur.

Joe and his helpers worked to get a good fire going, then called us all to supper—something he described as Native American tacos. It was a sort of deep fried flatbread the size of a dinner plate, and filled with a layer of beans in a spicy sauce, topped with diced tomato, lettuce, onion, shredded cheese, and a big wedge of steak on the side. I dug in hungrily but couldn't help noticing that Cody fed most of his to his new best friend, who seemed to have a whole family of furry best friends keen to share the bounty.

Once we were full and sleepy with contentment, the entertainment started. Joe introduced some of the helpers who turned out to be efficient multi-taskers, one playing a flute-like instrument, and another singing. Then the drums started, and the joy in Cody's face was highlighted by the flickering flames, and completely contagious, as he pulled us all up to dance with him.

The primitive, passionate beat swirled around us, making me dizzy and light-headed with the noise and movement and happiness blooming inside.

Then Cody drew me into his arms and kissed me soundly, ignoring the whoops and hollers as his body curved around mine. When he stood up straight, he looked very pleased with himself. All I could see was his beautiful face, and the night unfolding overhead, filled with a million stars, shimmering like diamonds against the deep black sky.

"Perfect," he murmured, his lips whispering against my overheated cheek.

We said goodnight to our fellow adventurers and headed for our sleeping bags.

"We could zip them together," I offered, hesitantly. "For warmth."

Cody raised an eyebrow. "For warmth?"

"Yes."

He winked at me. "Sure, why not?"

We kicked off our boots and I hoped I'd remember to shake them out in the morning. We'd been warned that scorpions liked to crawl inside them. Ugh.

I shucked my jeans, but left everything else on, then ogled openly while Cody unbuckled his pants and allowed them to slide down his long legs.

Unfortunately, I wasn't the only person able to enjoy the show. Even though we were a little way away, Joe had warned us to stay in sight of the campfire. He didn't say why, but the hungry howl of a coyote ensured I didn't ask any dumb questions.

I scooted into our joined sleeping bags, shivering in the cool night air. Cody slid down beside me, automatically wrapping his arms around my body so my head was pillowed against his firm chest.

Even though I could see every star in the sky, the powerful shadows of the mesas played tricks on my eyes, and I snuggled into his side, the solid warmth reassuring.

He sighed contentedly.

"If I'd known how good this feels, I'd have put this moment on my wish-list," he breathed.

"I wish I could spend a lifetime just like this," I said, happily.

He paused before speaking again.

"Maybe we can make a lifetime from this moment."

Then I felt him press a kiss into my hair.

I woke several times in the night, the soft sand surprisingly uncomfortable as the temperature dropped further. Each time Cody shifted subtly, his eyes gazing at me, then pulling me in closer, our shared warmth chasing the cold away.

We both lurched awake when Joe honked the jeep's horn, his version of our 5AM alarm call. My heart hammering unpleasantly, I rubbed the sleep from my eyes and turned to see Cody's warm expression.

"Sleep well, pretty girl?"

"Best sleep ever," I lied, rubbing my back to iron out the kinks. "How about you?"

"Oh yeah! Definitely best sleep ever—even though I didn't sleep much."

"Why not?"

"Too busy looking at you."

"Oh."

That deserved a kiss, and I didn't care about morning breath or the soft rub of stubble from his chin and cheeks or the fact that we were still in public.

Eventually, his large hands gripped the tops of my arms, and he levered me away.

"What's wrong?"

"Nothing. Just, um, getting a little too excited," he said, raising his expressive eyebrows.

"Oh." What was it about this man that left me with the vocabulary of a two-year-old? "I guess we should get up."

"You first," he coughed slightly. "I need a minute." And then he muttered under his breath, "I've been up all night."

My whole body flushed scarlet as he sat there grinning at me.

"Don't forget to shake out your boots, pretty girl."

The sky was lighter now, gray replacing the silky black, and the bright moon was slowly sinking behind the Hogan.

Drowsy from lack of sleep, I pulled on my jeans and boots, smiling to myself when I saw Cody's eyes glued to my legs. I couldn't help returning the favor, grinning to myself as he turned his back shyly.

His cheeks were pink when he looked up, and I smiled to myself as I helped him pack away our sleeping bags.

Joe herded us into the jeeps, and we tore off down the valley, the fresh wind whipping against our faces and through my hair as we raced the sunrise.

When the jeep jolted to a halt, we leapt out and struggled up a massive sand dune, then stood silent, hand-in-hand, watching color leak back into the world, until the sun rose, a fiery, blood-red, painting the mesas with a blaze of orange and gold.

"That was..." I couldn't find the words.

Cody hugged me tightly.

"A new day," he murmured, to himself.

The heat began to gather as the sun swept higher, reminding us that the desert in summer was not for quitters.

Joe honked the horn again to summon us, and we slid down the dunes like a couple of kindergarteners, spitting out mouthfuls of sand, and shaking it from our hair. I definitely got the worst of that deal, because Cody just brushed a hand through his, whereas my wild mop wouldn't be tamed this side of a shower and bottle of conditioner.

Joe grinned at us then pointed over his shoulder, and we saw the outline of horses walking toward us, led by a dark, saturnine man with wide, deep-set eyes.

Cody was first to greet the horses, gently rubbing their noses and sharing his breakfast cereal bar with them. They whickered and tossed their manes at him, before pushing their shaggy heads against his shoulder, trying to summon more food.

My horse was named Nastas, which meant 'fox tail', and Cody's horse was Niyol, or 'the wind'.

Nastas was squat and ugly with one wall-eye. I approached him slowly as he glowered at me balefully. I half expected to be bitten or bucked off, but Nastas stood there placidly as Cody helped me into the broad, western saddle, where I sagged uncomfortably like a sack of potatoes. I envied his graceful ease as he swung a long leg over Niyol, settling into the saddle as if he'd been born there.

"I thought you said you'd ridden 'once or twice'. Something you want to tell me?" I asked, quizzically.

"Three years of junior rodeo," he admitted, with a shy smile.

"So you were good?"

"Not bad."

"Why did you give it up?"

He shrugged and looked away. "Life happened."

I waited for a further explanation, but none was forthcoming, and Cody was saved further questions by Joe signaling that we were heading off.

The horses plodded along in Indian file through the uncompromising heat. The air was bone dry and their hooves kicked up small puffs of dust as they walked. It could have been a hundred years ago or five hundred years ago, and only the clothes and the horses' metal hooves had changed.

As the morning passed in a haze of sweat and sun, we explored Big Indian Spire, Castle Butte and other stops along the Mitten trail, my irritation at Cody's continuing silence melting away with the grand and rugged beauty of the ancient landscape.

We stopped several times to take photographs, posing with the cluster of sandstone buttes, soaring a thousand feet into the sky, letting our voices echo among the stones, and I wondered how far those sounds could travel. It felt like forever.

When we remounted, we slowly wound our way through the towering and silent rocks.

Last stop was Grandman Yatzi's hogan, an octagonal wood and mud-built hut.

A tiny woman, whose face was creased and lined like the valley she lived in, greeted us in Navajo, welcoming us to her home.

Joe translated.

"Grandma Yatzi can speak English, but these days it's easier for her to speak her own language. She will give a demonstration of traditional yarn spinning. If you have any questions while she works, feel free to ask her."

There was a nervous murmuring as we all wondered who was going to go first. The old lady's eyes, black as beetles, watched us, humor hinted at in her flat gaze.

Her crabbed hands began to spin, and Joe kept a narrative of the techniques she was using, describing the sheep the wool had come from, and how dye was fixed into the yarn.

When Grandma Yatzi was finished, she looked up and pointed a bony finger at me, the knuckles swollen with rheumatism and age.

As she beckoned me forward, I threw a nervous look at Cody.

"Grandma would like to braid your hair," said Joe.

I knelt in front of her and she combed my hair with her gnarled fingers, laughing huskily when she shook sand out of it. Then she wound the newly-spun yarn into my hair, turning it into a long and colorful braid down my back.

A childhood memory filled my eyes with tears, and Joe spoke with slow emotion.

"Grandma says your mother used to do this for you."

"Yes."

"But not for a long time now."

"No."

"Grandma says your mother watches you, and will see you again one day, but not for many, many years."

I couldn't speak. Cody knelt next to me and held my hand, squeezing my fingers tightly.

The old lady patted me on my shoulder, then laid her hand on Cody's cheek.

"She says you will begin your journey soon and that you know this," Joe intoned.

Cody nodded, his eyes still on me.

Joe cleared his throat.

"Grandma says to tell you that love can last many lifetimes."

"Yeah," said Cody. "I've been figuring that out."

He turned and placed a soft kiss onto my braided hair, making the other women in the group swoon quietly.

A little embarrassed, I clambered to my feet with Cody's help, and muttered a shy 'thank you' to Grandma Yatzi.

As we rode away, she stood stiffly and raised her hand in a silent farewell. Cody smiled and both of us waved.

Arriving back at the campsite and tourist shop was like suddenly sliding into 2014 from a quieter, slower century. It was something of a shock.

We grabbed a quick sandwich for lunch, said goodbye to Joe and the others, then headed back to Cody's truck. With luck, we'd be back in San Diego shortly before midnight. I was aware that we'd be leaving something magical behind.

We took turns driving, swapping every two hours to try and keep ourselves awake. Cody looked exhausted and I wondered how much he'd slept the night before. With the stubble on his cheeks and the dark rings under his eyes, he looked older than 18. Mind you, I was no oil painting. I was dusty and dirty, with sand in my hair and other unmentionable places. I was longing for a hot shower and my own bed.

Cody drove the last leg, kissing me awake as he parked outside my apartment.

"Oh, I was fast asleep then," I groaned, stretching my back and rubbing my eyes.

"I think I was, too," Cody admitted. "I just happened to be driving at the same time."

"Do you ... do you want to come up?" I asked, suddenly shy.

He looked thoughtful and my heart sank.

"Yeah," he said, at last. "I'd really like to come up."

I couldn't help the smile that spread across my face and he grinned back at me. Then I leaned forward, grabbed his t-shirt in my fists, and kissed the hell out of him.

"I guess that was the right answer," he chuckled against my lips, when we both came up for air.

"I guess it was," I agreed, my heart light.

We climbed out of the truck and walked toward my door.

I jumped when I heard a familiar voice in the darkness.

"Why are you home so late, Ava, and who is this boy?"

I turned around, wishing with all my heart that this wasn't happening. But no: he was real enough.

"Dad! What are you doing here?"

My heart began to pound, and I glanced at Cody, whose face wore an unfamiliar expression of gravity as his left hand clutched mine tightly.

"Good evening, sir. My name is Cody Richards. I'm a friend of your daughter's."

"I can see that," said my father angrily, ignoring Cody's outstretched hand. "I've been watching you maul her for the last five minutes."

"Dad!"

Cody ignored his rudeness and turned to me, holding my face between his palms.

"Do you want me to come in with you, Ava? Explain things?"

I kissed him sweetly.

"No, that's okay. Dad and I need to have a long talk. But thank you."

"Can I ... can I call you tomorrow?"

"I'll hunt you down if you don't."

He laughed sadly.

"I'll hold you to that, pretty girl."

He brushed a soft kiss over my lips, ignoring my dad's furious huff of disapproval, and climbed wearily into his truck. He smiled, waved once, and was gone.

"We have some talking to do, young lady," threatened my dad.

"Yes, we do," I agreed. "There are some things I need to say to you."

CHAPTER NINE

Dad and I talked for two hours. Well, maybe 'talked' isn't the right word. He shouted, I yelled. He barked, I roared. When he insisted I go back to Fayetteville, I refused. He ordered, I refused again. Then he begged and pleaded, and I tried to explain.

"I need to make my own decisions, Dad, good and bad. I won't always get it right, but that's how I'm going to learn. You have to let me make these choices."

"Even when coming to San Diego has been nothing but a huge mistake?"

"I don't see it that way, Dad. I'm managing on my own. I won't say it's been easy, because it hasn't."

"And this new 'maturity' that you insist you have, your refusal to come home to your family, it's nothing to do with this boy you've met?"

Ah, he had me there.

"Partly," I admitted at last, ignoring Dad's triumphant glare. "Cody has become important to me. He's taught me that life isn't something to take for granted; it's a privilege and I have to make the decisions that are right for me."

"Very profound," he sneered. "And what does he do, this boy?"

"As I said, his name is Cody, and he's important to me, Dad. Please respect that."

Dad was silent for a few seconds, then he said in a more conciliatory tone, "What does he do?"

"He volunteers at a homeless shelter."

For a moment, Dad was nonplussed. I knew what he was thinking: minus points for not having a paying job; plus points for the volunteer work.

"That's hardly a career," he said, at last.

"Not everything is about money. This is about giving something back to the community," I said firmly.

Our eyes locked.

"Are you going to come home?"

"My home is here, Dad."

He looked so shocked and upset that I almost caved, but I knew that if I went back with him, I'd regret not trying to stand on my own two feet.

"Dad, I don't say this to hurt you, but I've been your little girl for so long that you haven't wanted to see that I've grown up."

He sighed. "There is some truth in that."

I smiled and reached for his hand. "I met a real live Navajo medicine woman today."

"You have been having some adventures lately," he smiled, sadly.

"Yes, I have. Grandma Yatzi made this braid for me."

"It looks pretty."

"Thank you. Grandma Yatzi told me that she knew Mom used to do this for me."

He sucked in a sudden breath.

"She said that?"

"Yes. Isn't that amazing?"

"I do remember your mother doing that," he said, softly. "She spent hours fussing with your hair."

"And she said that Mom was watching me, from the stars, just like you used to say."

I felt his hand tremble.

"You're so like your mother," he said, his voice edged with warmth and sadness. "So full of life. I could never tell her anything either."

Tears pricked my eyes even as we shared our laughter.

Eventually, my dad left; back to his hotel and to the red-eye flight that he'd take by himself in the morning. I promised to phone him more often, and he promised to do his best to let me live my own life.

We hugged, and then he was gone.

When I woke up the next morning, the sun was high in the sky and it was almost midday. Grumbling to myself, I staggered out of bed, but not before realizing that the sheets were full of sand.

Sighing, I pulled them off the bed and trudged down to the laundry room. Then I had the longest shower in history and fortified myself with coffee and toast, before dragging my wearing backside into work.

The day passed slowly, even with an afternoon and evening shift at the coffee shop, but swapping texts with Cody kept a smile on my face.

I explained what had happened with my dad, and he said he was proud of me. I was kind of proud of myself, too.

As I only had to work until lunchtime the next day, he suggested a picnic at the beach.

That sounded all kinds of perfect to me.

Cody picked me up in the early afternoon. After a good night's sleep for once, I was feeling almost human again.

I thought Cody still looked a little drawn and I wondered if he'd lost weight, but he was freshly shaven and smelled of my favorite spicy cologne. He was dressed in board shorts and an old t-shirt that strained across the muscles of his chest. In other words, he looked delicious.

His grin was so wide that I could see that cute dimple popping out. Oh, I was going to have some fun with that later. I'd made up my mind.

He aimed for a light peck on the lips when I climbed into

his truck, but what he got was a full on lip-mashing, tongue-tangling, breath-panting, hands-groping San Diego 'hello'.

His face was flushed when I pulled away, his eyes dark, and when he licked his lips, I could see that my assault had left them slightly swollen. I felt rather proud of myself—as well as uncomfortably turned on, although Cody's condition was more obvious than mine. I couldn't help checking out his 'condition'; it was impressive.

Now I was the one licking my lips.

Cody cleared his throat.

"That was ... wow. I guess that was what you call good afternoon."

I smirked at him. Normally he was so composed, but now he looked downright flustered.

"That's just for starters," I said, buckling myself in.

He groaned softly and shifted uncomfortably in his seat.

We sat for a moment.

"I thought we were going to the beach?" I commented, at last.

"We are," he said, dryly. "As soon as some of the blood in my body returns to my brain."

"Oh," I giggled. "Sorry."

"No, you're not," he challenged.

"No, I'm not. Do you want me to drive?"

He shook his head, took a deep breath, and started the engine.

I hadn't been to the beach at La Jolla Shores before, but was glad that I hadn't, because it meant that it was another first for both of us.

We parked at the top of the hill, and Cody shouldered a large bag full of food and drink, while I carried one of his sleeping bags to use as a blanket. The hill sloped steeply for a short distance, fringed at the top by palm trees and shrubs. Soon, we were looking down onto a pale crescent of sand, anchored by a pier at one end.

It seemed to be a place favored by active beachgoers, and I

could see people swimming, paddling out on kayaks, and even a few surfers, although the waves were small and mellow today.

Cody found us a quiet spot in the hollow of a dune a short walk from the water's edge. I spread out the sleeping bag and collapsed onto it, smiling up at him.

His eyes were hidden behind sunglasses, so I couldn't tell what he was thinking, but he looked like he wanted to say something.

I held out my hand to him, and he dropped the bag of food onto the sand and stretched out next to me.

Sighing contentedly, I laid my head on his chest and stroked his stomach. Cody wrapped his arm around me, rubbing slow circles onto my shoulder.

"Being with you, like this," Cody began, his voice gruff. "I feel ... I feel..."

He swore under his breath, frustrated that he couldn't get the words out.

"Hey, it's okay," I said, leaning up to look at him. "I feel it, too. You don't have to explain. Let's just enjoy today."

"I can do that," he said, smiling softly.

I dipped down to kiss his full lips and then he captured my body, tugging me on top of him.

Eventually, our rough kisses calmed, becoming gentle and loving, instead of heated and bruising.

I sat up with a happy sigh and started unbuttoning my uniform blouse. Cody's eyes watched my fingers' downward progression. When I slipped it off to reveal my bikini underneath, I half-expected his eyeballs to pop out of his head and go rolling down the beach. He seemed paralyzed watching me, so I made a show of unbuttoning my shorts, then threw them in his face as I ran to the sea.

I heard his muffled yelp behind me, but made the mistake of looking over my shoulder as he yanked off his t-shirt and came charging toward me.

I let out a squeal and tried to run away, but he caught me around the waist and we both fell sideways.

I shrieked as the chilly water engulfed me, the sound ending with a gurgle as I swallowed a mouthful of ocean.

Then I felt Cody's hands around me, pulling me upright. Water poured from my body as I coughed and spluttered. Cody was laughing helplessly as he picked a piece of seaweed out of my hair, his skin sparkling as water dewed on his chest.

That moment—that was one I wanted to fix in my memory bank of special days. The brilliant blue sky, the warm sun, and Cody's eyes happy and laughing, and so full of love. It took my breath away.

"I love you," I said.

His smile froze.

"What?"

"I love you, Cody Richards."

His head dropped toward his chest and my heart stuttered, taken aback by his reaction.

"You weren't supposed to love me," he said, his voice oddly pained.

I laughed nervously. "Well, tough! Because I do."

He didn't say anything and couldn't even look at me.

"Well, this is awkward," I said, forcing myself to hold back my imminent tears.

I'd already turned away and started walking when he caught my arm.

"I'm sorry," he gasped. "I'm sorry … I just…"

"It's okay," I said, numbly.

"No! Fuck, no! It's not okay. God, Ava, I love you so much and I'd give you the world if I could, but…"

I caught onto the only words that mattered.

"You love me?"

His words shuddered to a halt.

"Yes," he said, gazing into my eyes. "So much. I love you, Ava, so much."

And that was another precious moment that I'd never forget: the moment that Cody said he loved me.

We held each other in silence, the shallow water rippling around our knees.

That day held so many special moments after our murmured words of love.

We swam in the sea, walked along the beach holding hands, ate ice creams, dozed in the sunshine, our arms and legs tangled together like two puppies. It was as if we were building a lifetime of memories in that one day.

As the sun began to sink, we gathered driftwood and built a campfire, shielded by the dune from the soft breeze that sprang up.

And then, shrouded by the gathering night, we made love.

It started with a touch, the smallest brush of his fingers against mine when he passed me a piece of wood to toss onto the fire.

Sparks shot into the air and I watched them for a moment before turning toward him, resting my hand on the warm skin of thigh, just above his knee, and just below where the material of his boardshorts ended.

"Be with me," I said.

He closed his eyes as if he was in pain. "Don't ask me, Ava, because I won't be able to say no, and I know I should."

I knew what he meant, because he was going away and didn't want to start anything.

He was wrong, of course; we'd already started something and I didn't want it to stop.

"Be with me now," I repeated. "Now is what matters. Isn't that what you've been saying to me? That each moment is precious?"

I moved my hand higher up his thigh, under his shorts, and he moaned softly.

I reached across with my other hand, sliding my fingers up his bare chest, over the thick ridges of his muscles, feeling his ribs beneath his smooth, satiny skin.

I kneeled up, both hands reaching around his neck, stroking the soft hair at his nape. Leaning closer, I nuzzled his cheek, brushing my nose across his jaw, then licking up his neck to his earlobe and biting gently.

He exploded into movement, his hands everywhere, pulling

me toward him—touching, tasting, molding, squeezing, stroking.

He was rough at first, his eagerness making him clumsy, his lips bruising mine. Then he gentled, his mouth murmuring my name against my heated skin, trailing hot, wet kisses across my breasts.

"So beautiful," he whispered. "So soft."

He slid the straps of my bikini from my shoulders, kissing the sun-reddened skin tenderly. His hand shook as he raised it to my breast, cupping it gently, swallowing my moan of pleasure as his tongue lapped against mine.

His free hand fumbled behind my back, trying and failing to undo the catch. I reached around and snapped it open, my breasts spilling free. He gasped slightly, then bowed his head, pausing as if seeking permission, then running his tongue around my nipples, warming, wetting, heating, tugging them with his teeth.

Desire built up inside me, pulsing softly, and I gripped his hips, my fingers digging into the skin covering the bone. When I pushed my hands under the waistband of his shorts, he hissed with pleasure.

He sucked on my neck and my bare breasts pushed into his chest as I arched my back to his touch.

Raising his head slowly, he cupped his hands around my face.

"Tell me again," he pleaded. "Say what you said."

My mind was spinning from his touch and his taste, trembling with want. I knew what I wanted, but I also knew what he *needed*.

"I love you," I repeated. "So much."

A soft cry escaped him, and his lips were on mine again; asking, taking, answering.

I pushed him backwards gently, until he was lying flat against the sleeping bag. His chest was rising and falling rapidly, and the bright moon highlighted his cheekbones and the hollow of shadow beneath.

I leaned forward, my hands braced on either side of his

body, and kissed up his stomach to his chest. He quivered with every touch, panting breaths escaping him as his hands hovered over my back, tentatively stroking my skin.

As I rose up his body, he took my breast in his mouth, suckling eagerly until I was a wet, moaning mess plastered across him.

He rolled me gently onto my side, my right hip digging into the sand, my left thigh dragging over his waist.

He was warm and solid between my legs, grinding softly against me. Then his fingertips danced along my spine, drawing heat to the surface wherever he touched. He toyed with the material at the edge of my bikini bottoms, again asking permission.

"Yes, touch me. Touch me everywhere."

His fingers eased lower, and my body arched suddenly as he reached the wet heat between my legs. He rubbed gently at first, then with increasing speed and force as my body convulsed around him.

His eyes were wide, watching my face as I came.

I rolled onto my back, gasping as Cody peppered my chin and cheeks and neck, spoiling my breasts with long, languid kisses as I floated back to earth.

"No," I said, quietly.

His body was suddenly tense. "No, what?" he asked warily.

"No, we're not finished," I said, huskily. "Not by a long shot."

I wriggled out of my bikini bottoms and tossed them behind me. Then I reached over to grip the erection that tented his shorts. His whole body shuddered and he closed his eyes.

I thought he was going to argue, but the moment I slipped my hand inside his shorts, he lost the power of speech. He was smooth and hard, solid and silky, twitching restlessly against my palm.

I pulled his shorts down and he helped me by raising his butt from the sleeping bag, and kicking them free.

I explored his body with my hands and tongue, learning

every dip and curve, every hard muscle and soft tissue, every ticklish spot, and the places that made him moan and sigh.

And then I took his long, thick shaft in my mouth, and when I peered up, I could see the tendons on his neck as he clenched his teeth.

A fine sweat broke out across his body, making his skin glow in the orange firelight.

He fought his own impulse to grip me hard, his hands digging into the sleeping bag and twisting it in his fists.

Realizing he was about to come, I slowed down, licking one last time before kneeling up and straddling his hips.

"I don't … have … anything," he gasped, as I smiled down at him.

"You don't need anything," I said, kissing his parted lips. "I've taken care of it."

I slid down on top of him, gasping slightly at the fullness, the connection, the searing touch of a man inside me—of Cody inside me.

His large hands grabbed my hips and he bent his knees, giving me better traction. I moved hard and fast and selfishly, wanting to a feel everything at once. My belly fluttered, a tightness and lightness flickering along my spine. Stars above and stars below, my body moved blindly, finding a punishing fluidity as we crashed together.

Cody's body heaved beneath me and I cried out. His own sob muted and astonished.

I collapsed on top of him, my hot breaths dampening his skin. His arms swept around me and he hugged me tightly.

"I love you," I gasped, as his arms squeezed me tighter.

We lay together, a tangle of arms and legs, relaxed in body and soul. My fingers drew lazy patterns on his hipbone and Cody sighed contentedly.

"I never knew," he said, kissing my neck.

"What didn't you know?"

"How good that would feel."

I paused in my happy mindless stroking.

"That was your first time, wasn't it?"

He coughed out a laugh. "Was it that obvious?"

"No," I said, truthfully. "It was really good. I'm just surprised that no girl ever snapped you up before."

And although I didn't admit it, I was giddy with pleasure that I had been his first.

"But the evening isn't over," I said, "unless you want it to be."

He shook his head slowly. "I never want this evening to be over. Ever." Then he paused. "It'll be my birthday in a few hours."

"What?" I was shocked and a little hurt that he hadn't mentioned it before. "Why didn't you tell me!"

"I wasn't planning on celebrating it," he said, simply.

"But this is a big deal! Now you're only three years younger than me."

He laughed softly. "I like being your boy toy."

"Good, because I want to do that again," I said.

And we did, sleeping, waking, making love, the whole night long.

Dawn was approaching as we finally left the beach, exhausted and satiated.

Cody drove slowly to my apartment, feeling the same reluctance I felt to let this perfect night end.

When he pulled up, he gripped my arms and pulled me toward him, kissing me deeply and desperately, unwilling, unable to let me go.

I felt tears in my eyes, and I didn't know why.

"I wish..." I began to say.

But Cody interrupted me. "No, don't wish for anything else. We had 10 wishes, and all of mine have come true. That's enough for me."

I kissed him again and again, and there was nothing left to say.

I climbed wearily out of the cab after ravaging his lips for one last time.

"I love you," I said.

"I love you to the stars and beyond," he replied.

CHAPTER TEN

I COULDN'T WAIT TO SEE CODY'S EXPRESSION WHEN I turned up with his favorite blueberry muffins. I know he'd said over and over that he didn't celebrate his birthday, but there was no way he was going to turn down freshly-baked muffins. Not when they were his favorites.

Even though I'd got home after dawn, I hadn't been able to sleep. The memories of the night before crowded through my mind; the way he'd touched me, the way we'd touched each other. Each kiss, each caress, every laugh, every second of a magical night. It had never been like that before.

I was still kind of amazed when he'd told me it was his first time. It was the one thing that didn't add up. How could a guy who was as hot as Cody, and as sweet, not have been beating girls off with a stick? I was more than happy that it had been me with him last night—but why?

Not that it mattered—not when what we had felt so amazing.

I was still smiling when I turned into his street.

I saw the police car first, and wondered if someone had been burglarized. But as I drove closer, I could see that there was an ambulance, too.

A cold feeling crawled up my spine, and I gripped the steering wheel tightly.

I had to park several doors down because the police car and the ambulance were both outside Cody's house. My knees felt weak as I climbed out of the car and hurried toward them.

A police officer stopped me, holding out her arm.

"You can't come in, miss."

"But my boyfriend lives here. Cody Richards. I have muffins," I said, stupidly. "It's his birthday."

The officer gave me a look of such sympathy that I began to feel desperate.

"Just a moment."

She turned away and spoke into her police radio. It spat and crackled, then she waved me forward.

A woman was standing at the door and I knew straight away that this was Cody's mother. She had the same black hair and striking pale blue eyes.

"Ava?" she asked.

I nodded dumbly, too choked to speak.

"I'm Sarah, Cody's mom. You'd better come in," she said, quietly.

I followed her into the living room and stood stiffly in front of the battered couch.

"What's going on? Is Cody okay? Where is he?"

Her shoulders began to shake and I knew, I just knew. She tried to speak but she couldn't, and then she put her hands over face and started to cry. I pulled her into my arms, this stranger who looked so much like the man I loved, and I held her.

And tears were pouring down my face, too.

We held each other for a long time before either of us tried to speak.

She passed me a tissue and we both half-laughed, half-sobbed, wiping our splotchy faces.

"Cody ... died this morning," she said, at last.

Even though I knew that's what she was going to say, I couldn't, *couldn't* believe it.

"What happened?" I asked, shakily.

She let out a long sigh, then turned to face me.

"Sit with me, Ava."

Exhausted and hurt, far, far from being cried out, with tears threatening to flow again, I sat next to her.

"Cody had cancer. He'd been fighting it since he was 13."

When I was 13, someone I knew well got sick with cancer—you could say it was a life-changing experience.

Oh, God! He'd been talking about himself.

"He had radiation therapy, and chemo seemed to beat it. He lost all his hair and missed a lot of school, but we thought he was getting better. He did for a while."

She sighed, and her face held unbearable sadness.

"But the next year it came back. So it was more hospital stays, more treatment—painful, invasive treatment. Cody's father couldn't take it and eventually he left us. Cody blamed himself for that, but really his father just didn't have the strength to watch his son suffer anymore. Some days, neither did I. But Cody was so strong, such a fighter."

I nodded slowly. "He wanted to live."

Sarah gave a small smile. "Yes, he did. He wanted to experience life … before he died." She sighed. "He missed most of high school because he was so sick, but he insisted he wasn't going to be a drop-out and he got his GED. Any college would have been glad to have him. But he knew he was out of time."

He'd said it. He'd tried to tell me: *Life is too short to live with regrets.*

"The cancer came back again."

"Yes. For the third time. The doctors wanted to give him more treatments, more chemo. But Cody didn't want that. He said he'd had enough of hospitals, and that he wanted to spend his last few months enjoying life, not waiting for death. When I had the chance of a job in San Diego, he made me take it. He said it would be a new start for both of us, even though we knew he didn't have long to live. And he'd never even left Kansas."

I was crying again as she told her story.

"We didn't really have any friends to leave behind—too many years spent in hospitals, I suppose. Cody loved living here, by the ocean. And then he met you."

Sarah held my hand tightly.

"You made him so happy, Ava. I'd never seen him like that —like a normal, teenage boy, in love for the first time."

I made a small, choking sound, and she pulled me into her arms.

"He did. He loved you so much. These last two months ... I'm so grateful."

"Why didn't he tell me?" I sobbed.

"Because you gave him a real life that was nothing to do with sickness and hospitals. You loved him for himself. You did love him, didn't you?"

I nodded, but I couldn't get the words out.

I rested my head on her shoulder as the tears continued to fall.

"He decided a long time ago that when the cancer started to win, he was going to ... the phrase he used was 'take himself out of the game'."

"What?"

"Cody didn't want to go back to hospital. Ever. He'd seen enough of death; he knew exactly what to expect, and he didn't want that. So he'd collected the pills he needed to end things on his own terms."

"Oh my God!"

"No, no, no! Ava, he was happy. *You* made him happy. I saw him early this morning when he came home—he was glowing. He said he'd had a perfect day, and that being 19 was better than he'd expected. We laughed, and I was so happy to see him like that, because the doctors had told him that it would be a miracle if he lived to 19, but he proved them wrong, didn't he? He hugged me and told me that he loved me, and I think I knew then, but I didn't want to believe it." She paused, wiping her eyes. "When I woke up again, he was gone. He'd made his choice, Ava. His choice on his terms. He wrote you a letter."

I couldn't even speak. I looked up at her, my eyes aching as I took the envelope, opening it with shaking hands.

> **Hey Ava,**
>
> **I bet you're pretty mad at me right now.**
>
> **I'm sorry. I know that's kind of lame for what I've done, but I mean it. I'm sorry I lied to you. I'm sorry I hurt you. I was in deep before I realized what was happening.**
>
> **I know how selfish this is—not telling you, and for what I've done. But I just wanted to have one summer where I was normal. I didn't want you to look at me the way everyone has looked at me since I was 13 years old. I could be myself with you—or at least the person I would have been without the Big C. This summer has been the best of my whole life. Because of you.**
>
> **I tried so hard not to fall in love with you, but that was impossible.**
>
> **And last night! What can I say? Except that I didn't know it could be like that. Being with you—making love with you—I never thought I could have that. I never thought life could give me something so good. It was a perfect day, and the perfect end to a perfect day. No point trying to top perfection, right?**
>
> **And I got to be 19 after all. I never thought that would happen.**
>
> **It must seem like I'm quitting on you just when things are getting good. I hope you'll forgive me for that. I know Mom will fill you in on everything. She's pretty great. But what we had ... what you gave me ... I**

didn't want you to be the person who sat around watching me die, and that's what would have happened if I'd stayed any longer.

You were the person who made me live. I'm going out of here with a smile on my face, and that makes me a winner.

I never meant to hurt you and I know that I did. It's the only thing I regret, leaving you with that pain.

Ava, I know I don't have the right to ask anything of you, but I'm going to anyway: Don't be sad for me, because I'm really happy right now. I'm going out on a high note, and not everyone can say that. Live for me, pretty girl, because you have so much life in you, so much love in you. Live the biggest life you can. A good life. Do it for me, but even more ... do it for you.

I love you, Ava Lawton. Best. Girl. Ever.

Cody x

The words blurred as tears filled my eyes again, but then I saw a second piece of paper in the envelope: our summer wish list.

All the items had been checked off. All those crazy dreams that we worked our way through, one by one:

1. **Get a tattoo.** ✓
2. **Swim with dolphins.** ✓
3. **Get drunk and high in Tijuana.** ✓
4. **Have a star named after me.** ✓
5. **Ride through Monument Valley.** ✓
6. **Sleep under the stars.** ✓
7. **Jump out of an airplane.** ✓
8. **Meet a Native American medicine man.** ✓
9. **Help in a homeless shelter.** ✓
10. **Have sex on the beach.** ✓

But then I noticed that another 'wish' had been added to the list. It had been checked off and had a largely smiley face drawn next to it.

II. **Fall in love.** ✓✓✓✓ :)

EPILOGUE

Over 100 people showed up for Cody's funeral. Even though he'd only lived in San Diego for a few months, he'd made a big impact. It made me realize that it wasn't the quantity of a life that matters, but the quality, and the way you live it

There were dog walkers from the park, a bunch of people from the homeless shelter, neighbors, people he'd met in coffee shops and on the beach. Everyone seemed to want to remember a piece of the joy and love that he'd shared with them.

He was loved...

Which is why I'm standing with my boarding pass in my hand, waiting to fly 7,000 miles to Florence. I'm going to live my dream.

I'm going to Italy, and I'm going to learn Italian, and I'll be studying the History of Art in one of the most beautiful cities in the world. I'm going to do all the things that I was afraid to do before, because I've learned that life is precious, and each day matters. Each day, I'm going to choose to be happy.

Cody crashed into my life, like an ocean wave out of a millpond sea. He changed everything. And I miss him so damn much.

But then I see him. I think I see him. Across the crowds of people, swirling among the human river, a flash of blue eyes.

That smile, that love of life, a shock of black hair. I see him and then he's gone, somewhere in the sea of faces.

Gone but never forgotten. Because life is a journey, not a destination.

I rub the small tattoo on my wrist, and I smile.

THE END

REVIEWS

Reviews are love! Honestly, they are! But it also helps other people to make an informed decision before buying my book.

So I'd really appreciate if you took a few seconds to do that.

Thank you!

MORE BOOKS BY JHB

Series Titles
*The Education Series
An epic love story spanning the years, through war zones and more...
*The Education of Sebastian (Education series #1)
*The Education of Caroline (Education series #2)
*The Education of Sebastian & Caroline (combined edition, books 1 & 2)
Semper Fi: The Education of Caroline (Education series #3)

*The Traveling Series
All the fun of the fair ... and two worlds collide
*The Traveling Man (Traveling series #1)
*The Traveling Woman (Traveling series #2)
*Roustabout (Traveling series #3)
*Carnival (Traveling series #4)
*Gypsy (Traveling series #5)

The Justin Trainer Series
The bodyguard and the billionaire
Guarding the Billionaire (Justin Trainer series #1)
Saving the Billionaire (Justin Trainer series #2)

* *The EOD Series*
Blood, bombs and heartbreak
*Tick Tock (EOD series #1)
* Bombshell (EOD series #2)

**The Rhythm Series*
Blood, sweat, tears and dance
*Slave to the Rhythm (Rhythm series #1)
*Luka (Rhythm series #2)

Standalone Titles
Contemporary Romance
The Lilac Cadillac
Battle Scars
One Careful Owner
*Lifers
At Your Beck & Call
The New Samurai
Exposure

New Adult
*Dangerous to Know & Love
Dazzled
Summer of Seventeen

Paranormal
*The Dark Detective: Venator (Book #1)
*The Dark Detective: Paukúnnum (Book #2)

Novellas
Playing in the Rain
*Behind the Walls

Anthologies of Short Stories
*The Year Book Volume 1
*The Year Book Volume 2
*The Year Book Volume 3

Audio Books
One Careful Owner
(*narrated by Seth Clayton*)

On the Stage
Later, After: Playscript
Trailer

With Alana Albertson
Father Figure

* These titles are published in languages other than English. Please check Jane's website for details—and receive **a free short story every month** when you sign up for her newsletter :)

QR code for Jane's website

ROMANCE WITH STUART REARDON

My love co-author with these titles

Two book series - contemporary romance

*Undefeated

*Model Boyfriend

Three book series - romcom

*Gym Or Chocolate?

*The World According to Vince

*The Baby Game

Standalone

Survivor Love Island *(romcom)*

*Touch My Soul *(novella)*

WRITING AS BERRICK FORD

Police Thrillers, UK

Dead Water
Dead Man's Dive
Dead Reckoning
Dead Shore

www.berrickford.com